Dear Reader,

Welcome to the town of Hard Luck, Alaska! I hope you'll join me there to meet the Midnight Sons, their families, friends and wives-to-be.

The people I want to credit with the idea for this project are, in fact, fictional—they're Valerie, Stephanie and Norah, the three sisters I wrote about in the Orchard Valley trilogy (Harlequin Romances #3232, #3239, #3244). I loved writing those books, I loved the characters and the town and last but definitely not least, I loved the way readers responded to the stories.

So when Harlequin suggested this six-book project, I was thrilled. Soon after that, the town of Hard Luck, the O'Halloran brothers and Midnight Sons all came to life. Never have I worked harder on a project, nor have I enjoyed my research more. In the summer of 1994, my husband and I traveled to Alaska, and I fell in love with the state—its sheer magnificence, the warmth of its people, the excitement of life on the "last frontier."

Now I invite you to sit back, put your feet up and allow me to introduce you to some proud, stubborn, *wonderful* men—Alaskan men—and show you what happens when they meet their real matches. Women from the "lower forty-eight." Women with the courage to change their lives and take risks for love. Women a lot like you and me!

Love,

Debbie

Debbie Macomber is one of the most popular romance authors writing today. She's written more than seventy romances for Harlequin and Silhouette and several bestselling "mainstream" women's fiction novels. Not surprisingly, Debbie has won a number of awards for her books.

She lives in Washington State with her husband, Wayne, and their dog, Peterkins. They have four grown children—and they've just become grandparents! Debbie's thrilled with her new granddaughter, Jazmine Lynn.

Debbie loves to hear from her readers. You can reach her at: P.O. Box 1458, Port Orchard, Washington 98366.

Books by Debbie Macomber

MIDNIGHT SONS

DEBBIE MACOMBER

Ending In Marriage

Harlequin Books

TORONTO • NEW YORK • LONDON
AMSTERDAM • PARIS • SYDNEY • HAMBURG
STOCKHOLM • ATHENS • TOKYO • MILAN
MADRID • WARSAW • BUDAPEST • AUCKLAND

ISBN 0-373-03403-2

ENDING IN MARRIAGE

First North American Publication 1996.

Printed in U.S.A.

The History of Hard Luck, Alaska

Hard Luck, situated fifty miles north of the Arctic Circle, near the Brooks Range, was founded by Adam O'Halloran and his wife, Anna, in 1931. Adam came to Alaska to make his fortune, but never found the gold strike he sought. Nevertheless, the O'Hallorans and their two young sons, Charles and David, stayed on—in part because of a tragedy that befell the family a few years later.

Other prospectors and adventurers began to move to Hard Luck, some of them bringing wives and children. The town became a stopping-off place for mail, equipment and supplies. The Fletcher family arrived in 1938 to open a dry goods store.

When World War II began, Hard Luck's population was fifty or sixty people, all told. Some of the young men, including the O'Halloran sons, joined the armed services; Charles left for Europe in 1942, David in 1944 at the age of eighteen. Charles died during the fighting. Only David came home—with a young English war bride, Ellen Sawyer (despite the fact that he'd become engaged to Catherine Fletcher shortly before going overseas).

After the war, David qualified as a bush pilot. He then built some small cabins to attract the sport fishermen and hunters who were starting to come to Alaska; he also worked as a guide. Eventually, in the early seventies, he built a lodge to replace the cabins— a lodge that later burned.

David and Ellen had three sons, born fairly late in their marriage—Charles (named after David's brother) was born in 1960, Sawyer in 1963 and Christian in 1965.

Hard Luck had been growing slowly all this time, and by 1970 it was home to just over a hundred people. These were the years of the oil boom, when the school and community center were built by the state. After Vietnam, ex-serviceman Ben Hamilton joined the community and opened the Hard Luck Café, which became the social focus for the town.

In the late 1980s, the three O'Halloran brothers formed a partnership, creating Midnight Sons, a bush-pilot service. They were awarded the mail contract, and also delivered fuel and other necessities to the interior. In addition, they serve as a small commuter airline, flying passengers to and from Fairbanks and within the North Arctic.

At the time these stories start, there are approximately 150 people living in Hard Luck—a preponderance of them male....

CHAPTER ONE

TRACY SANTIAGO always cried at weddings. It embarrassed her no end because, for one thing, people might believe she wanted to be married herself. Yet nothing could be further from the truth. Tracy had high ideals and knew she was often opinionated on a variety of subjects, most of which related to women's issues. Any man she got involved with would have to understand that. So far, the men in her life had been a severe disappointment.

"Dearly beloved we are gathered together this day to celebrate the union of..."

Tracy lowered her head and struggled to hold back the tears. She was standing by Reverend Wilson in the small community church of Hard Luck, Alaska, as her friend and former client, Mariah Douglas, exchanged vows with Christian O'Halloran.

Almost two years before, the town had advertised for women—or, more accurately, had advertised jobs they'd hoped would bring women north. The O'Halloran brothers, owners and operators of a bush-plane business called Midnight Sons, had been the prime movers behind the plan.

In their eagerness to entice women to Alaska, they'd promised jobs, free housing and twenty acres of land if the applicants agreed to live and work in Hard Luck for one year.

"Do you, Mariah Mary Douglas, take . . ."

Tracy swallowed and tilted her chin at a proud angle, refusing to humiliate herself in front of the entire town— and even more importantly, in front of Duke Porter. The thought of him was enough to stiffen her spine and keep the tears at bay.

When she'd first read about the men in Hard Luck, Tracy had been suspicious. An article in the Seattle newspaper had described the proposal, which sounded far too good to be true. Experience had taught her there was no such thing as a free lunch . . . or free land.

Her one fleeting thought that summer morning had been to hope any woman who signed the contract would have an attorney look it over first. Heaven only knew what this rowdy bunch of bush pilots was up to.

Little did Tracy think *she'd* be the attorney reviewing the contract.

A month later, Mr. and Mrs. Rudolph Douglas made an appointment with the prestigious law firm where Tracy was employed. Tracy was assigned to meet with them.

It seemed the Douglases' daughter, Mariah, had been hired by the O'Hallorans as secretary for Midnight Sons, and the couple was worried. They asked Tracy to investigate the people responsible for luring their daughter north. They wanted her to study the contract, find a way to break it and bring Mariah safely home.

Tracy remembered how Mariah's parents had characterized their daughter—a gentle, fragile, gullible, naive and easily swayed by control-seeking men. They feared that their only daughter had made a terrible mistake. Pride, they suspected, was the only thing that kept her in Alaska. Tracy believed the Douglases were justifiably worried.

Mrs. Douglas had battled tears as she spoke of Mariah's decision to leave Seattle. Tracy was provoked to fury by the idea of a bunch of men taking advantage of young women, especially women like Mariah. She eagerly accepted the assignment and immediately made plans to investigate the matter. Within the week, she'd traveled to Hard Luck.

Hell-bent for leather, she'd been prepared to do battle for the rights of Mariah and the other hapless women. To her astonishment, what she'd discovered was a tight-knit community hard at work, forging a future for their families.

Tracy had interviewed the women who'd signed contracts with the O'Halloran brothers. She was more than a little surprised to find them content and even happy, despite the almost primitive living conditions.

An even bigger surprise had been Mariah Douglas. The woman was nothing like her parents had described. Gentle and softhearted, yes. Gullible and easily swayed, no.

For her part, Mariah was embarrassed by her family's insistence she return to Seattle. The very reason she'd applied for the job in Hard Luck was to escape her parents and their domineering ways. Alaska offered her the opportunity to forge her own life without their constant interference.

The Douglases had wanted to file a lawsuit against the O'Hallorans, but Mariah had refused to cooperate. And so the issue became a moot point.

"Do you, Christian Anton O'Halloran, take as . . ."

Out of the corner of her eye, Tracy caught sight of Duke Porter. He'd positioned himself on the bride's side of the church just so he could fluster her. Tracy would have bet her grandmother's cameo on that.

It was during her first visit to Hard Luck that Tracy
had met Duke Porter, one of the pilots employed by
Midnight Sons. Duke epitomized everything she disliked
about men. He was an opinionated, stubborn, chauvinist who had no qualms sharing his outdated views of
women.

Duke referred to women as "the weaker sex." He was
the type of man who resented any woman in a position of
importance. As for women in politics, she suspected he
didn't even think they deserved the right to vote! The
aptly named Duke Porter might look like the rugged hero
of an old-fashioned western; the trouble was he sounded
like one, too.

They'd clashed the minute they met.

The man was by far the worst redneck Tracy had met
in years. Every time she thought about him, she gritted
her teeth.

Instead of worrying about Duke, Tracy forced herself
to concentrate on the wedding ceremony. The church was
crowded with well-wishers as Mariah and Christian
pledged their lives to one another.

Tracy didn't think she'd ever seen Mariah look more
beautiful. She wore the serene expression of a woman
who knows she's deeply loved. A woman cherished by the
man to whom she's willingly surrendered her heart.

Mariah had loved Christian almost from the moment
she arrived in Hard Luck. It'd taken Christian well over
a year to recognize that he loved Mariah, too. Once he
had, though, it seemed the youngest O'Halloran brother
was intent on making up for lost time.

The couple was married two weeks to the day after
they'd become engaged. Their whirlwind courtship left
Tracy's head spinning. Even if *she* wasn't a romantic,

Tracy was charmed by the way Christian had rushed Mariah to the altar.

She didn't begrudge her friend's happiness. Or Christian's. But she firmly believed that kind of love wasn't meant for her, and the thought saddened her, although she wasn't completely sure why.

Christian O'Halloran hadn't been able to take his eyes off his bride from the moment Mariah had entered the church on her father's arm. The only word to describe Christian was besotted, and Tracy knew Mariah was giddy with happiness.

"Ladies and gentlemen, may I present to you Mr. and Mrs. Christian O'Halloran. Christian, you may kiss your bride."

There was applause as Christian drew Mariah into his arms and slowly brought his mouth to hers. The kiss lasted long enough for whistles and embarrassed giggles.

Following the ceremony, the wedding party moved on to the reception, which was being held in the largest building in the community—the Hard Luck school gymnasium.

Mariah had kept Tracy informed of the goings-on in town with her long newsy letters. Tracy suspected she knew more about Hard Luck than some of the town residents did. Between her visits and Mariah's letters, she found herself falling in love with the state of Alaska. And specifically Hard Luck, the unique little town fifty miles north of the Arctic Circle.

As soon as she arrived at the gymnasium, Tracy stood in the reception line with the other members of the wedding party to greet the long row of well-wishers. The first person to come through the line was Abbey O'Halloran, wearing an ivory-colored, lace-fringed maternity top.

"Tracy, it's good to see you again," Abbey said, hugging her.

"You, too."

Abbey looked wonderful. Radiant. Tracy knew it was a cliché to describe a pregnant woman as radiant, but Abbey *was*. She simply glowed with health, happiness, excitement. In her last letter, Mariah had written that the ultrasound showed Sawyer and Abbey would have a daughter.

As the reception line progressed, Tracy was surprised by the number of people she recognized. Many she knew because of her visits, but others she remembered from Mariah's letters.

Just when Tracy was beginning to think she might escape Duke Porter, he stepped directly in front of her. He flashed her one of his cocky grins, the kind of grin that suggested she should be thrilled to see him.

She wasn't.

Tracy stiffened instinctively. "Hello, Duke," she managed to say, unwilling to let him know how much he intimidated her.

"Tell me," he said, apparently not the least bit concerned that he was holding up the reception line, "were those *tears* I saw in your eyes during the ceremony?"

"I don't know what you're talking about," she returned tartly. The man possessed an innate talent for zeroing in on whatever made her the most uncomfortable.

"It seemed to me," he said thoughtfully, rubbing his hand over his clean-shaven chin, "that your eyes became suspiciously bright while Mariah and Christian exchanged their vows. Tears, Tracy? From a woman who's never been married? You must be close to thirty now, right?"

"I said you were mistaken," she said, leaning past him to greet the next person in line. Duke, however, stood his ground.

"You've never been married, have you, Tracy," he said. "I wonder why. Judging by the tears, you must be wondering the same thing."

"As a matter of fact, I haven't given the matter a thought," she informed him stiffly, angry with herself for taking his bait.

He appeared to digest this information for a moment, then added, "It would take an unusual man to marry a woman who obviously hates men."

"I *don't* hate men," she said heatedly, then clenched her hands at her sides, furious that he'd done it to her again. Duke Porter knew precisely what to say to enrage her. What enraged her even more was how easily she allowed her control to slip with this...this bush pilot. Some of the best-known attorneys in the King County court system couldn't get a rise out of her nearly as fast.

He chuckled softly, clearly pleased with himself.

"You're holding up the reception line," she snapped in an effort to get him to leave.

Duke glanced over his shoulder. "You're right. We'll continue this discussion later. And there'll be no escape then, I promise you."

He leaned forward as if to kiss her, and she jerked her head back. But her action didn't disconcert him at all.

"Tracy?" he whispered for her ears alone. "Don't forget, I owe you one."

"Owe me?"

"For that kiss," he reminded her. He wiggled his eyebrows suggestively.

She opened her mouth to question his sanity. The last man on this earth she was interested in kissing was Duke Porter.

"The kiss," he reminded her in calm tones, "that you had Mariah deliver. You owe me, you little trouble-maker, and I fully intend to collect."

Tracy felt as if the floor had opened up and she was falling through open space.

Months earlier, she'd asked Mariah to kiss Duke on her behalf and to tell him that it was from his favorite femi-nist. They'd meant the whole thing as a joke. And frankly she'd never expected to see Duke Porter again.

He smiled at her, but there was no amusement in his face. His expression said that she was about to receive her due.

Tracy swallowed uncomfortably. She had nothing to fear, she told herself. Duke was all bark and no bite. Her eyes held his, unwavering.

The person behind Duke cleared his throat, and Duke moved forward to offer his congratulations to the bride and groom.

Tracy's eyes followed him. She recalled the first time she'd met Duke and how she'd involuntarily reacted to the disturbing sight of his rugged sensuality. Duke was well over six feet, almost a full head taller than her own five-three.

He was muscular, as well, but she knew that his strength wasn't the result of working out at some gym with fancy equipment. He was a man who lived hard and worked harder.

His hair was straight and dark, a bit long in the back. He needed it trimmed, but then he had every time she'd seen him. From a distance his eyes looked dark, but on closer inspection she realized they were a deep shade of gray. Brooding eyes.

Tracy's own were brown, and she wore her hair short and curly. With her court schedule what it was, she didn't have a lot of time to fuss with her appearance. She frowned on women who used beauty instead of intelligence to achieve their goals.

Her wardrobe consisted of a number of business suits in grays and blues. A few casual clothes—jeans and sweaters. One fancier dress for those rare evenings when she participated in some charity function. And now, one rose silk maid-of-honor dress. Tracy would never have chosen such a traditionally feminine outfit for herself.

She'd always disdained feminine trappings, which she saw as pandering to men. From an early age she'd learned the disappointing truth—men were often intimidated by intelligent women. It hurt their pitifully fragile egos to admit that someone of the "weaker sex" might know more than they did. In her opinion, Duke was a classic example of this kind of man, and she refused to allow him to diminish her confidence. As the reception continued, Tracy managed to avoid him. She headed for the buffet and three of the pilots did verbal battle to see which one would have the honor of bringing her dinner. While the men argued, Tracy dished up her own plate. The three pilots watched openmouthed as she sat down and started to eat. The comedy continued as they rushed toward the buffet line and then hurried back to vie for a seat next to her.

Tracy had dated her share of men and been in several short-term relationships, but rarely had she had more requests than she could handle. This was certainly an aspect of life in Alaska she hadn't considered.

Just when she thought she was safe, Duke asked her to dance. Actually he didn't ask, he assumed. While her mind staggered, seeking excuses, he effortlessly guided her onto the dance floor.

Rather than cause a scene, Tracy allowed him to take her in his arms.

"I was watching you just now," he said, and his voice was almost friendly. Almost, but not quite.

Tracy said nothing. She'd endure this one turn around the dance floor and be done with him. She wondered if this was her punishment for asking Mariah to kiss him.

"I've finally figured out what you really need," he continued.

Tracy couldn't resist rolling her eyes. This should be good. To her surprise, he didn't seem in a hurry to tell her.

"You're one of those women who think because you've got a college education you're better than a man."

Tracy opened to her mouth to argue, then hesitated. This time she wasn't going to be drawn into one of those no-win verbal exchanges. He could say what he wanted, and she would keep her mouth shut.

"I bet you thought you were clever outsmarting Ted, Ralph and Jim, didn't you? I suspect you're used to having men compete for your attention."

Tracy wasn't going to correct him, that was for sure.

"It seems to me you're the kind of woman who needs to be tamed."

Despite her vow to keep her mouth closed, despite her determination not to become involved in a pointless argument, Tracy burst out, "Tamed? You think a woman needs to be *tamed?*"

"It won't be easy," Duke went on as if she hadn't spoken. "It'd take a real man, not one of those *sensitive* males you're accustomed to dating."

"I beg your pardon?" Fury poured through her like molten lava.

"I know just the kind of man you date, too," he said smugly. "The ones who're trying to get in touch with their inner child."

"I'd like you to tell Gavin that."

"I take it Gavin's your boyfriend?"

"If you saw him you wouldn't call him a boy," she taunted as he continued to lead her around the dance floor.

"Really. Describe him to me."

She had no intention of doing so, but soon found herself mentally listing Gavin's virtues—even though she was a long stretch from being in love with her fellow lawyer. Gavin was witty and fun and they'd had a good time together, but it wasn't a serious relationship.

"A caring sensitive guy, no doubt," Duke muttered.

"Gavin's a man of the nineties," she said curtly before she realized Duke had done it to her *again*.

Duke snorted. "A man of the nineties. I can picture him now."

"You've never even met Gavin," she answered, quick to come to her friend's defense.

"I don't need to," Duke said. "I can see him already. He's just your type. Before he knows it, you'll have a ring through his nose and you'll be leading him around to show all your fancy friends how powerful you are. But once you're bored with him, it'll be bye-bye Gavin."

The effort it took not to respond sapped Tracy's strength. "I know what your problem is, Duke Porter," she announced evenly. "You're living in the Middle Ages.

Talk about *me* being close to thirty and unmarried. What about you?''

"I don't have any desire to marry."

"Me, neither."

He snorted again as if he didn't believe her.

"That says a great deal, doesn't it?" she mocked him openly. "It's perfectly acceptable for you to remain single, but you can't admit a woman could have those same feelings."

"Since the beginning of time, women have battled to control men."

"I see it the other way around," she argued. "Men seem to think it's their God-given right to dominate a woman."

"God created woman to please a man."

Tracy groaned aloud. Duke Porter belonged not in the Middle Ages but back in the Dark Ages. "You mean pleasure a man, don't you?"

That slow easy smile of his slid into place. "That, too."

"I don't believe it." Although the music hadn't stopped, Tracy pulled herself free of his embrace and walked off the dance floor.

Duke followed her. "Just a reminder," he said when they reached the far end of the room. "I still intend to collect my due for that kiss."

"I didn't kiss you," she insisted.

"Yeah, but you wanted to. And you want it now."

"I'd rather kiss a rattlesnake," she assured him with her sweetest smile.

"No need," he returned flippantly. "You can kiss me, instead."

DUKE STEPPED BACK and watched as his friends buzzed around Tracy like bees around a rose in full bloom. It irritated him to see his fellow pilots, men he trusted and admired, taken in by a pretty face.

Hell, Tracy Santiago wasn't even that pretty. Cute, maybe, but that was about as far as he was willing to go. One thing he knew—he didn't like her.

Never had and never would.

Duke remembered the first time he'd met the attorney. He'd known instantly that Tracy Santiago wanted to make trouble for Midnight Sons and consequently for all of them. She was after the company, hoping to prove that his employers were exploiting women.

What a bunch of hogwash. Each and every woman who'd moved to Hard Luck had come of her own free will. True, the O'Halloran brothers had gone out of their way to give women incentives to move north, but there'd been no coercion, no sales pitch, no pressure. The women who'd stayed and become part of the community *wanted* to be here.

It hadn't taken long for the fancy Seattle attorney to arrive, looking for an opportunity to ruin everything. There was a woman with her own agenda!

Duke hadn't liked Tracy the first time they met. Afterward he should've simply forgotten her—yet he hadn't. Months after her visit, he was still dwelling on their quick fiery exchanges. No one had ever stood up to him like that, challenged him, and when he questioned her rights…well, to put it mildly, she gave as good as she got.

Their feud didn't end with her visit, either. Fate had pulled a trick on them both when he answered the office phone one afternoon and heard Tracy on the other end. The incident reminded him of everything he hated about her—and everything he *didn't* hate.

Mariah seemed to take pleasure in razzing him about his aversion to a certain female attorney. She tossed Tracy's name into conversations the way an enemy would toss a grenade.

Then there was the day Mariah had kissed him. Mariah! It hadn't taken Duke or any of the other pilots long to see the lay of the land when it came to *her*.

She'd set her sights on Christian the first day she arrived in Hard Luck. So nothing could have shocked Duke more than the time she'd backed him into a corner and laid a lip-lock on him that had sent him spinning.

Then she had to go and ruin it by explaining that the kiss was actually from Tracy Santiago. If ever there was an ego buster, it was having that shrew get the upper hand.

What bothered Duke even more was that he hadn't been able to forget that kiss. He couldn't help wondering what it would've been like had it really been from Tracy. If they became romantically involved.

The truth was, that thought scared the living daylights out of him. Any relationship between them would be ludicrous. No man needed that kind of grief. Not that there was much chance of it happening to Duke, with her living in Seattle and him in Hard Luck.

His father had tried making that kind of long-distance relationship work years earlier, and it had destroyed his family. His mother had hated Alaska. She'd stayed several years, then moved to Texas, where she had family and friends. His father had remained in Alaska, and within a couple of years they'd divorced. Duke had hated Texas and was soon living with his dad. The two of them had gotten along well. John Porter had never remarried, and Duke didn't blame him.

John had died several years back, and Duke rarely heard from his mother, who'd remarried and raised a second family. It was just as well, since they had little in common. He suspected he was an unhappy reminder of something she'd prefer to forget.

There was no denying that his own background had made him cautious—downright wary, even—about women and marriage.

Soon after the kissing incident, though, he'd let a friend in Fairbanks arrange a date for him. Generally he didn't bother with blind dates, but the daily flights to Fairbanks didn't give him enough time to meet women. His reaction to Tracy had led him to forgo his usual cautions.

Before long, he had a thing going with Laurie. She was divorced and had a couple of kids her husband took on weekends. They had a nice arrangement, he and Laurie. She wasn't interested in marrying again, she said, which suited Duke perfectly because marriage didn't interest him, either. He'd leave that sort of foolishness to his friends.

No, sirree, Duke wasn't going to let any woman rule his life. He'd seen what could happen. But then again, he wasn't opposed to the type of cozy setup he had with Laurie.

Unfortunately it hadn't lasted long. A few weeks into their relationship, Duke realized she bored him. A perfectly good woman was crazy about him, and it was all he could do to feign interest. If he raised his voice, vented a little steam, Laurie cried. Real tears, too. Every now and then, he'd say something outrageous just to get a rise out of her. She'd smile benignly and astonish him by agreeing.

Before long, Duke found himself making excuses not to see her. He even traded his flights a couple of times as an excuse not to fly to Fairbanks.

When he figured he was being unfair to her, Duke dropped by her house to put a peaceable end to their relationship. He'd expected her to plead with him to stay, to weep and tell him how much she loved him.

Ending relationships had never been easy. Despite what some might say, he hated hurting a woman's feelings.

On the flight into town, he'd rehearsed a little speech. One in which he readily accepted the blame for their breakup. He hoped she'd accept his apology and agree to let things drop. By the time he'd arrived at Laurie's, he'd felt ready for just about anything. But Laurie shocked him into realizing how unprepared he actually was.

As he stood outside her door, bearing flowers and looking like a fool, she offered him an embarrassed smile and introduced him to her new husband.

It irked the hell out of Duke to realize that all the while she was seeing *him,* she'd been involved with this other guy.

In retrospect, Duke found the situation funny, though at the time he hadn't been at all amused. He'd gotten angry, said things he regretted and quickly left, stuffing his flowers into the nearest trash can.

In the air, on the return trip to Hard Luck, Duke realized that Tracy would never lead a man on the way Laurie had. If she had something she wanted to say, it got said. Nor would she date a man on the sly.

Once he'd landed the plane and taxied into the hangar, Duke realized he'd come full circle. Tracy Santiago once again dominated his thoughts.

Just like she was doing today.

TRACY FELT as if she'd been granted a stay of execution. Following the wedding dinner and dance, she escaped Duke and slipped into the back room to help Mariah change out of her wedding dress.

Before long the wedding couple would be on their way. Sawyer and Abbey would fly them into Fairbanks for their wedding night. The following morning the newlyweds would leave for California to board a ship for a two-week Caribbean cruise.

With tears in her eyes, Tracy hugged the woman who'd become her dearest friend.

"Dreams really do come true," Mariah whispered. "For so long I thought Christian would never realize he loved me."

"He's like all men," Tracy kidded. "He just doesn't know what's good for him."

"Oh, before I forget I need to tell you about the flight scheduled for you in the morning," Mariah said as she reached for her wool coat and tossed it over her arm. "You should be down at the field before ten. And dress warmly."

"Don't worry, I will," Tracy said, not wanting to delay her friend.

"It might be September in Seattle, but here winter's setting in. The rivers haven't frozen yet, but we've already had plenty of snow."

All Tracy needed to do was look out the window to see that. Snow in September was foreign to her.

"Also," Mariah said, her eyes bright with happiness, "don't be surprised when I toss the bouquet your way. I fully expect you to catch it, too."

"What?" Tracy's eyes widened in mock horror. "Are you nuts?"

"Not at all. I want you to know this kind of happiness."

Tracy's smile faded. As an attorney, she all too often witnessed marriages that came to bitter ends. She'd shied away from commitment, for that reason and plenty of others.

"Let one of the other women catch it," Tracy suggested.

"Not on your life. This one's for you."

Tracy wasn't sure she should thank her.

"One other thing," Mariah said quickly.

"What?"

"Don't be angry with me," Mariah said in a soft voice. "I didn't have anything to do with this."

"How could I possibly be angry with you?" Tracy said, and impulsively hugged her again.

Mariah's answering smile was wan. "Duke's the pilot who'll be flying you into Fairbanks tomorrow."

CHAPTER TWO

"BEN, I THINK it's time we got you back to the house," Bethany Harris said, sitting down in the vacant seat next to him. The wedding reception was winding down now that Christian and Mariah had left.

"Already?" Ben Hamilton muttered, frowning. It seemed that he'd just arrived. He wasn't accustomed to having anyone fuss over him. It took some getting used to, but at least he was back in his own bed, which was a hell of a lot better than the hospital in Fairbanks. A man could die in a place like that. The doctor said he needed plenty of rest. Unfortunately he hadn't bothered to tell the nurses that. Ben swore they woke him up at all hours of the day and night for the most nonsensical reasons.

The open-heart surgery had left him weak as a kitten. It used to be that he could run the Hard Luck Café from dawn to dusk and still have enough energy at night to play cards or read and watch a little television. Not anymore. Now he slept for much of the day; he didn't like it, either.

The doctors and Bethany had assured him that before long he'd be good as new. Ben hoped that was true, because he didn't make a good patient. Ask any of the nurses who'd been assigned to him!

"How are you feeling?" Bethany's question interrupted his thoughts.

"Fit as a fiddle," he said, gently patting her arm. It was difficult to believe he'd fathered this beautiful young woman. He hadn't known about her until she'd arrived in Hard Luck a year earlier. Talk about surprises! Learning he had a child had been the biggest shock of his life. Bethany had tracked him down and taken a job at the community school in order to meet him. She still taught there; she was married now and expecting her first baby—and she loved living in Hard Luck.

Ben was delighted with this opportunity to know his daughter. She was truly a gift, a miracle for a man who'd given up believing in such things a long time before.

Until Ben's recent heart attack, only Mitch, Bethany's husband, had known of the special relationship between them. Ben had figured the O'Halloran brothers suspected something, but they'd never asked and he'd never said. Now, though, everyone knew. And that was fine with Ben.

"Let me walk you back to the café," Bethany suggested.

It was hard to have someone constantly watching over him. The first few days he was home from the hospital he'd stayed with Bethany and Mitch in their home. That was about as much tender loving care as he could take.

Over their protests, he'd insisted on returning to his own place above the café. Mitch had carried up his bags, and Bethany had prepared the place, vacuuming and changing linens, even arranging a bouquet of late-blooming wildflowers. She worried about the stairs that led up to his apartment, but he'd managed them without difficulty, taking it slow and easy.

True, he didn't make the trek down to the café often, but he'd regain his strength in time and get back to work. It wouldn't be soon enough to suit him.

Ben's jaw tightened every time he thought about the revenue he was losing by keeping the café closed. More important, he knew folks around town depended on him for good food at a decent price.

Despite all the weddings taking place, the majority of the men in town remained unmarried, and many regularly came to the café for their meals. From the day it had opened, Ben's place had been the social center of the town.

"You ready?" Bethany asked.

Ben would've liked to stay a bit longer and enjoy the festivities, but he didn't have the strength to argue. He stood and Bethany looped her arm through his.

"I'm thinking about opening the café," he said, and before she could object, he added, "part-time of course."

"No way."

He should've known a child of his would be stubborn, but he'd counted on her at least hearing him out.

"Just for dinner."

"Don't even think about it, Ben."

He recognized that tone of voice. It was the same one he used himself when he refused to budge on a matter. Yup, her stubbornness was definitely an inherited trait—inherited from him!

"What are you smiling about?" she asked.

He'd been found out. "Nothing," he muttered, tamping down his grin.

As they left the reception, Bethany stopped to tell Mitch, her husband, where she was headed. Chrissie, Bethany's stepdaughter, was busy with the other children, and after a brief conversation with the girl, Mitch joined his wife. One on either side of Ben.

Ben hated feeling helpless, but he let Bethany and Mitch support him until they arrived at the café. The place was empty and cold, a stark contrast to all the times it had been filled with the talk of men and the clatter of dishes. What Ben wouldn't give to crank up that grill and fry a few burgers!

Because he was drained from the afternoon's socializing, he took the stairs one at a time. He didn't like admitting how weak he felt, but Bethany and Mitch seemed to know without his saying a word.

"Sit down and make yourself at home," Mitch said, urging him toward his favorite recliner.

"I *am* at home," Ben snapped, then immediately regretted the outburst. "It feels good to have my own things around me. I—I appreciate your concern."

Mitch accepted the apology by giving him a gentle pat on the shoulder.

There was a certain solace in being home, among his familiar comforts. The recliner. The television with its antenna, one spoke wrapped in aluminum foil. He'd gotten a satellite dish a few years back, but hadn't bothered to remove the antenna. You never knew when it might come in handy. His glance fell on the American flag framed and mounted on the wall. A small memento of more than twenty years spent in the navy serving his country.

It wasn't much, but this was home and the place he loved.

"Help yourself to something to drink," he told Mitch, gesturing toward the refrigerator in the compact quarters. To his surprise Mitch took him up on the offer.

These days the couple generally stayed only long enough to be sure he was comfortable and then were on their way. Ben didn't blame them; their lives were busy. He didn't need anyone to tell him he wasn't good company.

Bethany claimed the chair across from him, and Mitch sat on the thick padded arm, his hand resting on his wife's shoulder. Come spring, Ben reminded himself, there'd be a brand-new baby at their house.

The thought of their child, his own grandchild, was one of the things that had helped him through the worst part of his recovery. He wanted to live to see Bethany's children. He'd missed out on the chance to be a father, and by golly he looked forward to being a grandpa.

"Mitch and I wanted to talk to you about the café," Bethany said, glancing at her husband.

Ben tensed. He should've realized there was something coming. If these two thought they were going to convince him to retire and sell the café, they'd better have another think.

"I'm not selling," he said, unwilling to have them even broach the subject.

"Sell the café?" Bethany repeated. "Ben, no, we'd never suggest that!"

His shoulders relaxed as relief eased through him.

"We only want to encourage you to hire some help."

"I planned on doing that myself as soon as—"

"You got around to it," Bethany finished for him. "You've been saying that for months. Here you are, recuperating from open-heart surgery, and you're still just talking about it."

"Yes, well..."

"Look at you. You're barely out of the hospital and already you want to open the café."

"Part-time," he said under his breath, knowing they weren't in any frame of mind to listen. They'd already made up their minds, the same way he had.

"Just how long would that part-time business last?" Bethany asked in a knowing voice. Ben suspected she was right. He'd open up the café for dinner, and soon people would start wandering in around lunchtime, and before he knew it, he'd be back on the same old treadmill. But it was what he loved, what he did best. Fact was, he longed for his friends. People used to come in every day for coffee and conversation, and he missed that more than anything. Hell, he was downright lonely.

"People count on me," he explained.

"We know that." At least Mitch agreed with him. "That's why we want you to hire someone to come and help *now*. Someone with plenty of experience you won't need to train."

"Just where do you suppose you'll find someone like that?" Ben asked. He wanted it known right then and there that he didn't think much of their idea. "Especially with the kind of wages I can afford." His mind leapt into overdrive. Another cook, especially one with plenty of seasoning, would run the place *his* way. Pretty soon Ben wouldn't belong in his own kitchen any more!

"I've already talked to Matt and Karen about taking in a boarder and—"

It hit him then. Amazing how long it took him to catch on. Bethany and Mitch already had someone in mind.

"Who is it?" he asked outright, interrupting Mitch.

Once more the couple exchanged glances. "Mrs. McMurphy," Mitch said.

"A woman?"

"Do you have something against a woman, Ben?" Bethany asked, challenge in her tone.

He opened his mouth to detail exactly why he *did* object to a woman working in his kitchen, then realized he couldn't say one word and not offend Bethany.

"Where'd you find her?" he asked, instead.

"In Fairbanks. She cooked for a number of years at the Sourdough Café. Christian and Sawyer go there a lot, so they met her. She told them she's looking for a change of scene."

Ben knew the Sourdough Café had a reputation for good food. His objections started to dwindle. "She won't want to work here in Hard Luck," he muttered. The kids meant well, he knew.

"Why don't you meet her and ask her yourself?" Bethany suggested. "I talked to Sawyer, and he said Mrs. McMurphy could fly in with the mail run one day next week. If you don't like her, then no harm done."

He wasn't going to like her, but Ben didn't have the heart to burst the kids' bubble. Just because the woman could cook didn't mean he was comfortable letting a stranger into his kitchen.

"You'll at least meet her, won't you?" Bethany pressed.

"Okay, okay," Ben answered reluctantly. "But I'm not making any promises."

TRACY WAS the first one out at the airfield the following morning. Fat flakes of snow drifted down from a leaden sky, and she wondered if the flight would be canceled because of the weather.

She lugged her suitcase into the mobile office for Midnight Sons, and the first person she saw was Duke. He appeared to be reading something on a clipboard; he didn't look up or acknowledge her. Not that she expected he would.

Sawyer O'Halloran was there, as well, talking into the radio, and from the sounds of it, he was collecting the latest weather data.

When he'd finished, he turned off the switch and swiveled around to greet Tracy. "Looks like it'll just be you and Duke."

This was not promising. "What happened to Mr. and Mrs. Douglas? It was my understanding we'd be leaving together."

"They've decided to stay on another day," Sawyer explained. "Mrs. Douglas doesn't want to fly in the snow."

"Will the storm be a problem?" Tracy asked.

"Not as far as we can tell, and Duke's the best pilot in our fleet. You don't have anything to worry about," he said, then mentioned casually that the plane had recently been serviced. This, she suspected, was done in an effort to reassure her that everything was shipshape.

Duke's gaze met hers. "You want to wait with the Douglases?" he asked. Although there was nothing in his voice, a glint of challenge flashed from his cool gray eyes.

"No, I'll go," she said. Really she had no choice. Her court schedule was packed and she could ill afford to miss work.

"What time's your flight out of Fairbanks?" Duke asked.

She told him, and he glanced at his watch. "Then let's leave now. If we're lucky we'll be able to avoid the worst of the storm."

She reached for her suitcase. Duke paused, his gaze holding hers. "You aren't afraid of a little snow, are you?"

"Of course not," she returned stiffly. Somehow, it seemed important not to let him know she didn't entirely trust him *or* the weather. But the truth was, she'd prefer to fly when the weather was clear.

His eyes revealed his approval. "You ready?" he asked, setting aside the clipboard.

"Sure," she said brightly, forcing some enthusiasm into her voice.

Duke headed out the door, and she guessed she was supposed to follow him. But she didn't, not right away.

"Sawyer," she said, gripping her suitcase with both hands.

The middle O'Halloran brother looked up from his desk.

"I just wanted you to know that...that I think you've been completely fair with the women you've hired." This was more awkward than she'd thought. For some time now, she'd wanted to apologize, set the record straight, and this was the first real opportunity she'd had. "I realize we started off on the wrong foot, what with me arriving here the way I did. I couldn't be happier for Mariah and Christian, and the others."

He cracked a smile and dismissed her apology with a wave of his hand. "Don't worry about it. You were only doing your job. The Douglases are decent people, and they had every right to be concerned about Mariah."

Tracy felt better for having shared her regrets. They'd weighed on her mind all weekend. She'd meant the O'Hallorans no harm. Over the past year she'd come to respect the three brothers, and she didn't want there to be any hard feelings.

"I'd best be on my way," she said, glancing over her shoulder toward the door. "I had a marvelous weekend. Thank you."

"We were pleased you could make the wedding on such short notice."

It had taken a bit of finagling, but Tracy had managed to change her schedule. This was one wedding she hadn't wanted to miss, even though it meant traveling more than twenty-five hundred miles.

Duke was inspecting the outside of the plane when Tracy joined him. "You can get in," he instructed absently.

"Thanks," she muttered, more certain than ever that this one-hour flight would feel like a lifetime. She'd taken Mariah's advice and dressed warmly in wool slacks and a thick cable-knit sweater. Since the interior of the aircraft was heated, she couldn't decide if she wanted to keep her coat on or take it off.

Tracy was about to ask, but decided the less conversation between her and Duke the better. Since he wore his jacket, she'd wear hers, as well.

Once inside the aircraft, Tracy fastened her seat belt and held her breath. Flying didn't usually frighten her, but she'd rarely flown in a storm or in an aircraft this small. Neither Sawyer nor Duke had expressed any qualms, though, and they were the experts. Midnight Sons was proud of its safety record, and she was confident they wouldn't fly if conditions were hazardous.

Duke climbed into the plane and started the engine, which fired readily to life. Next he reached for the headset, adjusting it over his ears, and spoke into the small attached microphone. She could barely hear him above the roar of the engine.

They taxied to the end of the runway, then turned around. She watched him do an equipment check, pushing various gauges and buttons. According to Sawyer, Duke was the best pilot they had. This ride wasn't going to be a lot of fun, with the snow coming down fast and furious, but the weather didn't seem to concern him, so Tracy decided she shouldn't worry about it, either. Easier said than done...

The engine noise increased dramatically as Duke boosted the power and raced down the snow-covered gravel runway. Soon they were airborne. A few minutes later, Duke removed his headset and tucked it beneath her seat. After that, he glanced in her direction once, as if to check on her.

"I'm fine," she shouted. But he must've known she was afraid from the way she kept her hands tightly clasped in her lap.

It came to her that if she was willing to put her differences with the O'Halloran brothers behind her, she should be willing to do the same with Duke. The words, however, stuck in her throat.

With Duke it was...personal. Duke felt a woman needed to be tamed. Indeed! It was time the man woke up and realized he lived in the twentieth century. Good grief, almost the twenty-first!

She supposed that nothing she could say or do would change his opinions, and it would be useless even to try.

Sighing, Tracy closed her eyes and tried to sleep. Not that it would be possible, but if Duke assumed she was asleep, he might ignore her.

Tracy wasn't sure when she noticed a difference, but at one point she became aware that something wasn't right. It seemed, to her uneducated ear, that the engine noise had altered slightly. She opened her eyes and straightened to find Duke studying the instrument panel.

"What is it?" she asked, studying the gauges herself.

He gave no outward indication that anything was wrong. She might not have known if it wasn't for the increasingly odd noises the engine made.

"Duke, don't play games with me!" she cried. This was no time to pay her back for that silly kiss—and yet she hoped that was exactly what he was doing.

He looked at her as if he didn't know what she meant.

"Okay, so I had Mariah kiss you," she said, and didn't care that she sounded frantic. "I admit it was a stupid thing to do. I ... I don't know why I did it, but if you're trying to retaliate and frighten me, then I—"

It was as though he hadn't heard her. He cursed loudly.

"What's wrong?"

The engine sputtered, and there could be no denying they were experiencing some kind of trouble. Big trouble.

"We're losing—"

The engine faltered again.

"Start looking," he ordered tersely.

"For what?"

"A place to land. We're going down."

No sooner had he spoken than the engine quit completely.

CHRISTIAN AND MARIAH sat outside their gate at the Fairbanks airport waiting for their flight. Christian's arm was around his wife's shoulders.

His wife.

The realization took some getting used to, but it was a good kind of adjustment. Mariah tucked her head under his chin, and he stroked her hair contentedly.

"Our flight should be called soon," he told her. An entire two weeks on a cruise ship with his bride sounded like heaven. His life had been turned upside down in the past three weeks. A month ago he would've laughed at anyone who suggested he'd be married by the end of the month. Yet here he was, and about as happy as any man had a right to be.

Mariah's eyes were closed, but she was smiling.

She had good reason to be tired and happy. Their wedding night had been one of discovery and joy. Christian was still shocked that he'd been so dense about his feelings for Mariah all these months. Once he'd recognized that he was in love with her, it was as if his whole world had expanded.

For the first year of their acquaintance, he'd barely been able to work in the same room with her, convinced she was nothing but trouble. Everyone else was crazy about her, but ironically, she *was* trouble—for Christian's heart.

He'd sensed that his self-contained emotional life was about to be blown wide open. Knowing he was in grave danger, he'd raised a protective barrier against her. He'd been ill-tempered, unreasonable and cantankerous, yet she'd put up with him day after day.

It would take him a lifetime to make up for the dreadful way he'd treated her, but it was a task he accepted willingly.

"Christian," she murmured, her eyes still closed. "Why'd you assign Duke to fly Tracy out of Hard Luck?"

Christian grinned. Tracy and Duke. Those two were like fire and ice. Opposites in every way.

"They don't get along, you know," Mariah said, as if he wasn't already aware of the fact.

"Don't get along" was putting it mildly. He wouldn't be surprised if they argued the entire flight. He could picture it now. Duke would start the argument because he thrived on verbal battles. Christian suspected he particularly enjoyed getting Tracy riled up. Then she'd respond, and soon the fur would fly.

"It seems like cruel and unusual punishment to subject those two to each other for any length of time," Mariah added.

"Your parents will be there to mediate," he said, then kissed the crown of her head. "Have I told you yet how much I love you?" he asked, changing the subject.

A slow satisfied smile spread over her beautiful face. "As a matter of fact, you did. I love you, too."

His arm tightened briefly around her shoulders. "I know." Her love was one thing he'd never doubt.

"By the way," she said, raising her head to meet his gaze, "when did you start drinking your coffee black?"

Christian figured heaven would bless him for the restraint it required not to laugh outright. As his secretary, Mariah had served him coffee every morning for more than a year. Some days she added cream, others sugar, occasionally both, but only rarely did she get it right.

"Just recently," he answered.

His heart swelled with love, and he wondered if it would always be like this with him and Mariah. Sawyer seemed to indicate that it would. He'd married a year earlier and had never been happier. Charles, the oldest brother, had gotten married last spring.

At the time, Christian had felt light-years away from making a commitment to any woman, yet here he was, less than six months later, with his new wife by his side. The best part was how happy he was. He'd always thought that when the time came to marry, he'd go into the relationship with a storehouse of regrets, knowing his bachelor days were over. It hadn't been like that marrying Mariah. He felt like the most fortunate man alive.

He wondered what he would've thought had he been able to look into the future the day of Charles and Lanni's wedding. He probably would've run screaming from the church.

What a fool he'd been. What a complete and utter fool.

"You never did answer my question," she said, nestling her head more securely against him.

"What question?" He was easily sidetracked these days.

"About assigning Duke to fly Tracy into town.."

"I didn't assign him the flight," Christian murmured.

She lifted her head enough to meet his gaze, her eyes filled with unasked questions.

"It's true," Christian assured her.

"But I saw it on the schedule myself. I went so far as to warn Tracy and assure her it wasn't my doing, and now you're telling me Duke *isn't* flying Tracy into town?"

"No," he said, and laughed smugly, "I'm telling you I didn't *give* Duke the assignment."

"Then how—"

"Duke requested it."

"He did?" Her wonderfully expressive face revealed her shock.

Christian nodded. "I thought it was a bit strange myself. But who am I to question such matters?"

"Really." Mariah's smile was back. "So Duke requested it. I'm beginning to suspect there's more to those two than meets the eye."

Christian opened his mouth to argue, then changed his mind. Everything he knew about love and romance he'd learned from his wife. She was the expert.

AVIATE. NAVIGATE. Communicate.

The words raced through Duke's mind at laser speed. His first response was to take whatever measures were needed to restart the plane's engine. From the way the oil pressure was falling, Duke guessed the line had ruptured. The engine sputtered to life a couple of times and then died with a final spurt. Nothing he did could restart it, despite his continuous efforts.

"What do you mean we're going down?" Tracy sounded close to panic. He wanted to reassure her, but he didn't have time.

"We'll be making an off-field landing," he shouted. And then, because he knew she was frightened, he added, "They happen all the time."

"Maybe they do for you. You *have* done this before, haven't you?"

"Plenty of times." He hoped the lie would keep Tracy from panicking. The truth was, he'd made only one emergency landing, years earlier, in conditions a hell of a lot better than this.

He reached for his headset and started talking, linking with the air-traffic controller in Fairbanks, communicating his coordinates. He sounded calm, but his heart was beating so loudly he was sure it could be heard over the microphone.

As the plane descended through the clouds and the snow, it became more and more difficult to make out the terrain below.

"Duke..." Tracy grabbed his arm, her grip tight. He felt her terror, experienced his own.

"Look around," he ordered. "We need to find a clearing where we can land."

September and March. Every pilot in Alaska knew those were the most dangerous months in which to crash. Snow on the ground, and the rivers and lakes had yet to freeze over.

In another week he could have settled this baby down on a frozen lake. If he tried that now, they'd both be dead in a matter of minutes.

Fact was, he didn't know what their chances were.

Not good, he decided. Not even promising.

Because of the snow and the wind, the plane glided. He worked the rudder, manipulating the aircraft any way he could, hoping to navigate it.

"I...I can't make out anything below," Tracy said.

Duke couldn't, either.

"What should I do?" she asked, and once more he heard the panic in her voice.

"Hold on as best you can."

"I'm doing that already."

"You might pray," he suggested next.

"Pray...I don't think I know how. It's been a while."

He figured they were both about to get a crash course in the art of prayer. Crash course. If it wasn't so tragic, he'd have laughed.

As they drifted out of the sky, Duke glanced at Tracy and winked. "Hold on tight, sweetheart."

He was beginning to make out the contour of the land, and he silently cursed when he saw trees. This was the worst possible scenario.

"Right before we land," he instructed, straining to sound cool and collected, "open your window and the door."

"I'll fall out."

"No, you won't." Although controlling the plane required his complete concentration, he reached over and grabbed the end of her seat belt. He yanked hard, making sure it was as tight as possible.

Then he did the same with his own.

Out of the driving snow, a small clearing appeared. Working as fast as his hands would let him, Duke shut down the plane's electrical system, including the rudders. The last thing they needed on impact was a spark to set off a fire.

"Hold on, sweetheart," he shouted as the aircraft slammed into the ground. A tree tore off the right wing, and Tracy screamed and covered her face with both hands.

The plane spun, out of control, cartwheeling like a broken toy over the harsh landscape. Duke was nearly wrenched from his seat. A piercing pain stabbed his left arm as he felt the bone snap, and then he felt nothing.

CHAPTER THREE

TRACY WAS VICIOUSLY jolted from side to side. The aircraft slammed against the side of a tree and spun around. The entire world became a blur, colors blended, lights blinking. The oxygen seemed to be sucked from the air.

Tracy heard Duke cry out and at the same moment felt something hit her head. Warm liquid trickled down her face. Blood? A scream froze in her throat. It came to her then. She was going to die.

The incredible thing was that she felt no fear, no terror—nothing but a strange sense of peace.

Abruptly the tumbling aircraft crashed into something solid. The jolt was strong enough to nearly rip her seat from its hinges. The seat-belt restraints were the only thing that kept Tracy from being hurled through the front window.

Then there was silence. Total, absolute silence.

It hurt to breathe, and she struggled for each lungful of air. Her chest felt as if a heavy weight was pressing against her. She managed a raspy breath and choked.

The seat belt kept Tracy in an upright position. It was painfully tight, and she realized that was the cause of her distress. She needed every ounce of strength she had to release it.

"Duke." Her voice was a hoarse whisper as she turned her head to look at her companion. Her distress increased tenfold when she saw him. Blood flowed freely from a gash on the side of his head.

Tentatively she reached out and touched his face, not knowing if he was dead or alive. "Please, oh, please don't be dead. Duke, be alive. Please be alive."

Although she felt as if her arms and legs had been jerked from their sockets, her fears propelled her into action. She located the pulse in his neck and nearly sobbed with relief.

Next she twisted around in her seat and applied pressure to Duke's wound, which continued to bleed profusely. The cut was jagged and very deep. Even to her medically inexperienced eye, it was obvious that he needed stitches.

Every time she moved, her body screamed with pain. But she maneuvered herself around so that she was kneeling on her seat. Then she removed the scarf from her jacket and opened a package of tissues she found in her pocket; with these she constructed a makeshift bandage for Duke's head.

Judging by the odd position of his left arm, she knew it was badly broken, perhaps a compound fracture. She leaned her forehead against his shoulder, struggling not to weep with frustration and fear.

Duke groaned and rolled his head to one side.

Tracy's relief was so great she covered her mouth with both hands. "Duke! We're alive. We're alive!"

He opened his eyes and smiled when he saw her kneeling next to him. "I told you this'd be a piece of cake," he murmured.

"Where's the first-aid kit?" she asked. "Your arm's—looks like it's broken."

He closed his eyes and nodded. "Feels like it, too." His face was deathly white. His gaze narrowed as he studied her. Raising his good arm, he touched her face, his hand gently caressing her cheek. "You're hurt."

"No," she countered, "I'm fine really. You're the one who's hurt."

His hand came away covered in blood. "You have a cut..." His voice started to fade. Tracy feared he was going into shock.

"Duke, where's the first-aid kit?" She tried to remember the emergency medical class she'd taken her first year in college, but worried she'd forgotten too much to be of any help to either of them.

Duke told her, and she scrambled into the back, digging through the emergency equipment. She located two sleeping bags and several packets of brown plastic bags. These, she discovered, were something called Meals Ready to Eat. Or so the package claimed.

The first-aid kit was the last item she pulled free. Tucking the plastic box under her arm, she squirmed forward. By the time she arrived back in her seat, she was breathless and weak.

Duke's face remained white with pain. She thought of unwrapping one of the sleeping bags and covering him with that, but there was so little room. If only she could get to her suitcase.

"I've got the kit," she said, feeling triumphant for having accomplished this one small feat. Then she went about treating his injuries.

She unwound her scarf and examined his cut, relieved to find the bleeding had slowed. She applied new tissues and retied the scarf.

Next she had to deal with his broken arm. She removed the inflatable splint from the first-aid kit, then shuffled through the box, looking for painkillers. She groaned in frustration. There didn't seem to be any.

Duke rested his head against the back of the seat and closed his eyes.

"I don't think you're supposed to sleep," she whispered. Her fears were rampant. At least the bleeding from her own cut seemed to have stopped. Her injuries appeared to be minor compared to Duke's.

"I'm going to have to do something about your arm."

He offered her a lopsided smile. "Have at it, sweetheart. Anything you do isn't going to make it hurt any more than it already does."

Sweetheart. He'd called her that three times now, and in an unmistakable tone of affection. Always before, he'd said it in a caustic way, as if he meant to insult her.

"It'd probably be best if I got out of the plane and came around and worked on it from your side."

"No," he spit out the word. "Don't leave the plane... If anything happened, I wouldn't be able to help you." His protest seemed to drain him of what little strength he had left. His good hand clenched hers, cramping her fingers. "Promise me," he whispered breathlessly. "Promise me no matter what happens, you'll stay right here."

"I promise," she said.

He closed his eyes again and sighed audibly.

"Your arm . . ."

"It'll be fine."

"No, let me do what I can. If I crawl behind your seat, I might be able to get the splint around it. Please, let me try." It was the least she could do.

"All right."

Tracy climbed into the limited space behind him. In an effort to give herself more room, she climbed out his door and stood thigh-deep in the fallen snow. The cold and wind on the sensitive skin on her face and hands felt like tiny needles. She did the best she could to make Duke's arm comfortable, attaching the splint and inflating it, praying all the while that she wasn't hurting him more.

He bit off a groan.

"I'm so sorry," she whispered.

"Get back inside. Hurry now," he instructed. "It's too cold out there for you."

"I'm fine. It's you I'm worried about."

"I'll feel a hell of a lot better when you're right here beside me."

For the first time since the accident, Tracy smiled. Duke actually wanted her with him. From the very beginning, Duke had gone out of his way to challenge her, provoke her, tease her—and it had always worked. He irritated her faster than any man she'd ever known. But she realized now that she'd actually begun to look forward to their heated exchanges. Their arguments invigorated her. At the moment, though, an argument was the last thing she wanted.

By the time she climbed back inside the plane, she was shivering. Her fingers felt numb; she clenched and unclenched them in an effort to bring back feeling.

"I wish there was something I could give you for the pain."

"Don't worry," he whispered, dismissing her concern. "I'll be all right."

But she knew from his drawn pale face and harsh uneven breaths that he was in a lot of discomfort.

"I have some pills—they're like aspirin—in my purse. Would that help?" she asked. She didn't mention that the medication was actually designed for menstrual cramps.

Duke closed his eyes and nodded. "Couldn't hurt."

After a few minutes of awkward searching, she located her purse. She dug around until she found the

package, then fed him three tablets. He swallowed them
without water.

"Where are we?" she asked. Snow covered the wind-
shield, making it impossible to see out.

"Best I can figure, we're close to Kunuti Flats."

Not close enough, otherwise they would've missed the
trees, Tracy mused. Swallowing hard, she asked the
question that concerned her most. "How long will it take
for someone to find us?"

"Don't know. Not to worry…emergency locator beam
goes off immediately—links with a satellite network.
They know where we are. Someone's on the way… Radio, need to contact them by radio…"

Tracy could see that he was struggling to remain conscious. "Duke!" she cried, reaching for his hand, gripping it in both of hers. His eyes rolled and he slumped
forward.

Gently she eased him away from the plane's steering
device. Never had Tracy felt so alone—so helpless and
afraid. These were unfamiliar emotions for her, and she
fought to regain a sense of control.

The radio. Before he passed out, Duke had said something about the radio. She knew next to nothing about
how to use it. But she *had* to contact Fairbanks. When
they took off, she'd watched Duke speak into the microphone attached to the headset. She could do that,
couldn't she?

Careful not to disturb him, she removed the headset
from him and placed it over her own head.

"Hello," she said, trying to keep her voice cool.
"Hello, anyone there?"

Nothing.

In desperation she stared at the instrument panel. No
lights showed, and she was sure they had earlier, before

the crash. Obviously damage to the plane had been severe. Now what?

She felt surprisingly calm. She knew there had to be a way to reach help and forced herself to think clearly. She studied the panel with all its gauges and instruments; they meant nothing to her.

A two-position switch caught her eye. *Battery.* Stretching forward, she flipped it up. Lights flashed across the panel and a sense of exhilaration filled her. Static popped in her ears.

"Mayday. Mayday. SOS. SOS!" she shouted into the tiny microphone.

The static cleared and a voice returned, "Fairbanks radio, Baron two, two, niner five hotel. I'm approximately five zero miles south-southwest of reported position of distressed aircraft."

The man didn't seem to be speaking the same English as Tracy. "This is Tracy Santiago. I'm a passenger with Duke Porter out of Hard Luck. Our plane is down—we crashed. Duke thinks we're near Kunuti Flats."

Tracy heard another voice respond, and she realized he was talking to the man who'd spoken first. She was listening in on their conversation. The second man was on the radio in Fairbanks. But he didn't seem to want to talk to her. Once more, she started pushing buttons.

"Hello, hello. Help!"

A click sounded in her headset. She waited, remembering the old "Sky King" television reruns she'd watched as a child. She needed to press down and speak, then release the button for a reply.

She'd figured it out. A sense of jubilation shot through her. "Hello, someone answer me, please. Over." Sky King had always said "over."

"Radio calling, this is Fairbanks radio. You are on the emergency frequency."

She had the right place.

"Do you have an emergency?" the same voice asked.

"Do I ever! I'm with Duke Porter."

"Is your aircraft Cessna seven two eight bravo gulf?"

"How would I know?" she demanded impatiently. "How many planes do you people have that've crashed?"

"What's your status? Do you have injured?"

"Yes. The pilot's unconscious. Just get someone here, and quick. I don't know how badly Duke's hurt."

"What are his injuries?"

She told him what she could, and then answered what seemed to be an endless list of irrelevant questions, about supplies and what they were wearing and how she felt. Not once did he answer her one major concern—When would help arrive?

"We have your ELT signal. Suggest you turn off battery to conserve power," he instructed. "We had you on radar all the way down. Help will be dispatched, weather permitting."

"How long? Can't you at least tell me how *long* that'll be?" She prayed it would be soon, but she hadn't liked the gist of his questions, nor the suggestion that she turn off the battery to save power. His tone indicated she and Duke might be here for more than a few hours.

"Air Force Rescue copter will be dispatched as soon as weather permits," the man on the radio repeated.

"When will that be?" she cried, growing more frantic.

"Meteorological forecasts call for clearing in six to twelve hours. Conserve your warmth and battery power.

This frequency will be monitored continuously should you require further assistance."

"Thank you—but please do what you can to get here soon," she pleaded, her heart sinking. Then she flipped the switch and severed her contact with the outside world.

The silence was intense.

A thousand questions bombarded her all at once. She could survive another six to twelve hours, but she didn't know about Duke. He was in terrible pain and she could do nothing to help.

Fear and loneliness returned full force. Soon she was shaking with cold. She reached for a sleeping bag and wrapped it around Duke and herself, then sat back, closed her eyes and tried to think positively.

Six to twelve hours. That wasn't so long—not really. They'd be fine for a few more hours, wouldn't they? Sure, it was cold and scary, but together they'd make it. Perhaps if she said it often enough, she'd come to believe it.

Tracy felt herself growing tired. Duke weaved in and out of consciousness; she knew that by the way he breathed and sometimes groaned. She wanted to stay awake for him, watch his vital signs, but the lure of sleep tugged at her.

If she was to die, she'd be with Duke.

Strangely the thought comforted her.

SAWYER DIDN'T THINK he'd ever experienced such frustration. Duke was down, and what information he'd received so far was sketchy at best. For hours now, he'd been sitting by the radio, waiting.

Despite the storm, every one of his available pilots was in the air. He hadn't asked them to track the emergency locator beam; they'd volunteered.

Sawyer knew that John, Ted, Ralph and the others felt as if they were searching for family. His pilots were a close-knit group, and Sawyer was fiercely proud of each man.

Duke was popular with the others, a natural leader. They looked up to him and often sought his advice. He'd been with Midnight Sons longer than almost anyone. Sawyer valued him as a colleague—and as a friend.

But recently they'd come close to losing Duke; he'd threatened to quit. Threatened, nothing. In a fit of righteous indignation, Duke had handed in his notice.

Christian had been at the heart of the trouble. His brother had grounded Duke for a single flight, and the pilot had been furious. To this day Sawyer didn't know what had happened between them, but Christian had gone over to the bunkhouse and they'd somehow settled their differences.

Sawyer shuddered at the thought of Duke's leaving. The fact was, he considered Duke his best pilot—certainly his most experienced. If anyone could get out of this alive, it was Duke Porter. But then, Sawyer was uncomfortably aware that these kinds of decisions often weren't in a pilot's hands.

More than ten years earlier Sawyer had gone down in a plane himself. He hadn't been alone, either; he'd been with his father. Weather conditions had been bad, but a hell of a lot better than they were now.

Unfortunately that hadn't saved David O'Halloran. Before help could arrive, Sawyer's father had died in his arms.

Memories of that day flooded his mind, charged his senses back to those last moments when he'd watched the life ebb out of his father. The pain returned, as fresh now as it had been that afternoon. Sawyer rubbed his eyes, wanting to stop thinking, stop feeling. Forget.

Inhaling sharply as he tried to push the memories aside, he ignored the pain. But the scene remained steadfastly in his mind. Again and again it flickered like an old silent movie, frame after frame. Impotent rage and defeat came at him like a fist in the dark.

"Sawyer."

He gasped and whirled around to face his wife. His relief was instant. Abbey—his wife, his love, his salvation.

"Have you heard anything more?" she asked quietly. Her face was tight with worry.

"Nothing," he told her.

Abbey walked to his side and slipped her arm around his shoulders. Sawyer readily accepted her touch, needed her tenderness to help erase the memories. His fears for Duke and Tracy were overwhelming.

Sawyer placed his arm around Abbey's thickening waist. Touching her gave him comfort no words could express. That she was pregnant with their child was a second miracle for a man who hadn't expected the first.

She bent down and kissed the top of his head. "Everything will be fine."

"I hope so," he said. "From what I understand, the rescue team won't be able to reach Duke and Tracy until the weather clears."

"You mean they'll be stuck out there?"

"It looks that way. We don't have any choice."

Abbey tensed. "Why?"

"The chopper can't get to them in this storm."

"Does anyone know if they're hurt—or how badly?"

That was the question that plagued Sawyer the most. Surviving in the cold for any length of time was difficult enough, but with their injuries... "Tracy talked to the controller herself."

"Tracy?"

He nodded, unsure how much to tell her. He didn't want to alarm Abbey unnecessarily. "Duke appears to have sustained the worst of it," he said finally. "Cuts, bruises, broken arm. But there's also the possibility of internal injuries."

She pressed her cheek to his. "There's nothing you can do."

"I know," Sawyer murmured, and that was the worst of it. He had a gut full of anger mingled with guilt—for what, he didn't know. And fear. Yes. More than anything, fear.

It had been like this the day he'd lost his father, the day the light had gone out of his life. For years Sawyer had carried the guilt of that crash, although David had been piloting the plane. Afterward he was left to wonder if there'd been something, anything, he should have done, *could* have done, that might have spared his father's life.

He hadn't realized the extent of his emotional injuries until he'd met Abbey and married her. His wife's love had been a gift, a healing balm that eased away the self-recrimination.

"Tracy and Duke together," Abbey murmured. "Do you think they can last the night without killing each other?"

For the first time since he'd learned about the crash, Sawyer grinned. "You might have a point there."

WHEN TRACY AWOKE it was dark. Her eyes fluttered open and she realized her head was propped against

Duke's shoulder. She felt warm and almost comfort-able.

His good arm was around her.

"Duke?"

"So you're awake."

"You, too... I was so afraid. You passed out."

"You afraid?" She could hear the smile in his voice. "I didn't think you even knew the meaning of the word."

He must be feeling better if he was up to teasing her. "If I didn't know it before, I do now," she admitted shakily.

Concerned that she was hurting him by leaning against him, she shifted and attempted to sit upright.

"Stay," he said in a whisper.

Tracy wished she could see him properly. But if he was awake and not in obvious pain, that could only bode well.

"I'm not too heavy for you?"

"No." His face was so close his breath stirred the hair at her temple.

"Do you need any more... aspirin?"

"No, thanks. Save them for later. I'm about as com-fortable as I'm likely to get."

Her arm rested against his middle, and her head re-mained on his shoulder. "It's dark already. How long did I sleep? What time is it?"

"Three, maybe."

"The helicopter won't come for a while. I figured out how to work the radio." She couldn't help being proud of this. "Fairbanks seemed to think it would be six to twelve hours."

"I guessed as much. We'll be fine."

"You blacked out on me. I got on the radio and..."
To Tracy's amazement, her voice broke. She took a moment to compose herself, breathing deeply, but instead, her throat closed up and her eyes filled with tears.

"Tracy?"

She buried her face in his warmth and held back the emotion as long as she could. When it burst free, the sobs shook her entire body. "I thought you were dead! I didn't know what to do... alone. I was afraid of being alone."

His hand stroked her back. He murmured something, but so softly she couldn't make out what it was. But his message was clear; he offered her solace and comfort.

"I'm sorry," she whispered when the tears were spent. "I didn't mean to..." Embarrassed now, she wiped the moisture from her face.

"I was afraid, too."

"You?" Now that was something Tracy had trouble believing. The great Duke Porter. The man was fearless.

The wind howled outside the plane. From the side window, Tracy could tell that it had stopped snowing, but the sky was dark and ugly. She couldn't see any stars. The only light in the plane came from the moon reflecting off the snow.

"You okay now?"

"Yeah." But she wasn't.

"I've got a candy bar in my jacket. Want some?" he offered.

Now that he mentioned it, she realized she was hungry. "Sure."

In the dim moonlight, Duke retrieved the candy from inside his coat pocket and handed it to her. The chocolate bar was squashed and mangled.

"You might want to see if you can read the expiration date," he suggested. "I haven't a clue how long I've been carrying it."

At this point Tracy was too hungry to care. She peeled back the wrapper and broke off the top square. She gave it to him, then took a piece for herself.

Generally Tracy avoided sweets, and it had been a long time since she'd had a candy bar. Right now, she thought it was the best thing she'd ever tasted.

"You called me sweetheart," she said, breaking off the next piece. Her fingers stilled abruptly. What had made her say that? She hesitated, wondering if he was going to pretend he hadn't heard her, hoping he would.

"Don't take it personally." His voice had stiffened noticeably.

"I didn't. We were going down and I was close to panicking and you...you didn't mean it. Besides, I wouldn't want to upset your girlfriend in Fairbanks."

She felt rather than saw his gaze bore into her.

Every time she opened her mouth, her foot seemed to drive deeper and deeper into her throat. Whether he had a girlfriend in Fairbanks or anywhere else was none of her business.

"Forget I said that," she said hurriedly. Her face burned. Duke was a virile attractive man; it was logical that he'd be involved with someone. She'd wonder if he wasn't.

"How'd you know about Laurie?" he asked, his voice cool.

"Uh..."

"Mariah." He supplied the answer himself.

She didn't bother to deny it.

A tense silence followed. "I haven't seen Laurie in some time," he told her softly.

Mortified beyond belief, Tracy felt it was important to clarify the situation at once. "I didn't ask, really I didn't. Mariah mentioned one time—briefly, very briefly—that you had a friend you sometimes visited in town. She said it in passing."

"But you remembered?"

Tracy shrugged. She *had* remembered. The information had stuck in her mind for weeks. She hadn't questioned why. Now and again, she'd found herself wondering what kind of woman would interest a man like Duke. She'd wanted to think he was like other men she'd met who never looked beyond the size of a woman's breasts. But she'd always known that wasn't true of Duke. He might be a lot of things—a traditionalist, maybe even a chauvinist, a man who provoked her to anger—but he didn't see a woman as just a body.

"You were right about Gavin," she whispered. "He—he's hoping to find his inner child."

Duke laughed shortly.

Tracy found herself smiling.

"Laurie bored me."

"Bored you?" Tracy wanted details. The happy way her heart reacted to his words didn't bear considering.

"She agreed with me far too often," he admitted.

"The poor dear must have wanted to keep the peace," she teased.

Duke chuckled. "You, though—I always could count on you to find a way to challenge me."

"That's because you say the most outlandish things. Really, Duke, you've got to be more up-to-date."

"Nah," he returned. "And miss seeing your eyes spit fire at me? I've never known a woman who looks as pretty as you when she's roaring mad."

Pretty. It wasn't a word men used when they talked about her. Smart, yes. Tough. Hardworking. A good attorney. But rarely did men view her as pretty.

Once again her throat tightened, and she found herself struggling to hold back tears. She was lost somewhere in the Alaskan bush in a downed plane with an injured pilot beside her, and all she could think about was that he thought she was pretty.

CHAPTER FOUR

AS NIGHT CLOSED IN around them, Duke began to wonder if he'd make it. At times the pain in his arm was almost more than he could bear.

Tracy shivered at his side, but they were together. For a while, they talked, telling each other all kinds of things. Private things. Duke found it was like talking to his oldest and dearest friend. Comfortable. Comforting. He knew he was rambling but it didn't worry him, because he trusted her. He did worry about her bouts of shivering. As best they could, they conserved their body heat beneath the sleeping bag.

Duke's feet suffered the worst of it. The cold pierced through him like swords thrust into his legs. He'd dozed off, but the pain didn't let him sleep long. He'd lost feeling in his toes, which was, he supposed, a blessing of sorts. The relentless tingling sensation only added to his misery.

He was frightened for Tracy, who'd grown still and quiet.

"What if no one comes by morning?" she suddenly asked. It was the first time she'd spoken in at least an hour, he estimated. It was becoming more and more difficult to keep track of time.

"Don't worry, help'll be here soon." He sounded more confident than he felt. Duke had flown into plenty of storms and was well aware of their hazards. The last time he'd checked on the emergency frequency, there hadn't been any sign that the storm was breaking up. Apparently the cold front had moved directly over Fairbanks.

"Try to sleep," he urged. He couldn't sleep himself; the pain he was in was too great to allow him the luxury of that escape.

Tracy rested her head against his shoulder, nestling into his warmth, sharing her own. A swell of tenderness washed over him. He feared what would happen to her if he was to die.

Several minutes later he gauged by the even measure of her breathing that she was asleep. If he was about to die, he decided, the time had come for him to think about his life—analyze his regrets. Somewhat to his surprise, he realized he didn't have many. To his way of thinking, his sins had been few, his mistakes plenty. He wished his relationship with his mother was better. The fault, if there was one, lay squarely on his shoulders. He hadn't wanted to intrude in her life.

He'd never cheated anyone, rarely lied, and other than an occasional weakness of the flesh, he'd lived a good and decent life.

He wished he'd fathered a child. That came as something of a shock. A man didn't often consider his mortality. He dismissed the regret, certain it had occurred to him because of everything happening in Hard Luck. Weddings...and now babies. Karen Caldwell and Abbey O'Halloran were pregnant, and last he'd heard, so was Bethany Harris.

He didn't know what kind of father he'd be, but the thought of being one appealed to him.

A house appeared in his mind—a house that didn't exist. He'd always hoped to build his own home someday. Nothing fancy, but one that would suit his needs. He figured he'd live in Hard Luck, close to his friends, be part of the community. He'd regret never having a chance to build that house—if he was to die.

Tracy stirred, and he studied her in what little light the moon afforded him. He'd been astounded by the way she'd handled this crisis. He probably shouldn't have been, though; she was one hell of a woman. Almost against his will, he found himself admiring her, grateful for her cool head and gentle touch.

One day Tracy Santiago would make some lucky son of a gun a great wife. She'd be a great mother, too; he felt it instinctively. He pressed a silent kiss to the top of her head, then closed his eyes. Yeah, she was one hell of a woman....

A whooshing sound disturbed him, and he shook his head in an effort to clear his mind. He must have slept. Night had become day.

The noise came again; it seemed to be some distance away.

"Duke, did you hear that?" Tracy lifted her head from his shoulder.

He opened his mouth to tell her he did, but couldn't find the strength to speak. He was glad she didn't appear to notice that he was fading quickly.

"I need my suitcase!" she cried excitedly. "I know I promised not to get out of the plane, but I won't go far."

"No..."

"I'm going to get my red nightgown and climb onto the wing and wave it. They might not see us in the snow otherwise. I'll be careful," she assured him, and then she did something totally unexpected.

She kissed him. Sweetly. Excitedly. On the lips.

"The helicopter's almost here." Her voice was giddy with relief.

Duke hadn't the strength to tell her that the emergency locator beam would give the pilot their precise whereabouts. It was unnecessary for Tracy to climb onto the wing and signal. Even in his groggy state, he found the idea amusing.

The sound of the rescue chopper's approach sharpened as the aircraft drew near. Duke closed his eyes and whispered a prayer of thanksgiving.

Sounds began to mingle in his ears. The chopper, men's voices, Tracy's excited cries. Then someone was at his side and he was being extracted from the aircraft.

"Please be careful," Tracy shouted in the background. "Can't you see he's hurt?" Duke saw a flash of red and wondered if it was the nightgown she'd mentioned. Pity he'd never seen her in it.

Pain cut into his arm and he groaned as he was placed on a narrow stretcher.

"Don't touch his arm like that," Tracy yelled. "What's the matter with you people? Can't you see he's in pain?"

Duke closed his eyes. Minutes must have passed before he opened them again, because when he did, he realized he was in the chopper and they were airborne. An emergency medical technician worked over him, taking his vital signs.

Tracy sat on the other side and held his hand between both of hers. She didn't look good, he thought. Dry blood matted her hair. The cut didn't appear to be serious, but he noticed a goose egg of a lump on her head; he hadn't been aware of it earlier.

Nor had he known how pale she was.

"Tracy." Her name was all he could manage.

Her eyes brightened with tears and a few spilled over. "You're going to be fine. We both are... I don't know if we could've lasted much longer.'' She smeared the tears across her cheek and seemed to be embarrassed by them.

Although it required every last ounce of his strength, Duke brought her hand to his lips and kissed her knuckles.

He was barely aware of what followed. The next thing he knew, he was being wheeled down a hospital corridor. He couldn't remember landing or being taken from the rescue helicopter or driven in the emergency car. Nor did he know what had happened to Tracy. She'd been with him from the beginning of this ordeal, and he wanted her with him now, dammit. If he hadn't been so weak, he'd have asked.

He heard raised voices and recognized a few. Sawyer was there; so were John, Ralph and a couple of the others. They all seemed to be talking at once. He attempted to sit up to tell his friends that it'd take more than a little crash in a snowstorm to kill *him*. Unfortunately he didn't have enough energy to so much as roll his head.

Where the hell was Tracy?

"Tracy." He called her name, but the word came out little more than a whisper.

A man in a white coat leaned over him. "You're asking about your friend?"

He nodded.

"You don't have a thing to worry about. She's fine— a few bruises, a couple of cuts, exposure. Dr. Davidson is examining her, but she's giving him all kinds of trouble." The physician grinned. "It seems she's worried about you. I told Davidson to tell her you're going to be fine once we get that arm set. It's a compound fracture, which makes it a bit more complicated. We'll be taking you into surgery within the hour. I've given you something for the pain, so you should be able to rest comfortably.''

That was what he was feeling, Duke realized, the absence of pain. Tracy was all right; he could let go now.

SAWYER WAITED until he'd had a chance to see Duke and Tracy personally before he searched out a pay phone to call Abbey. He knew she'd be anxiously waiting to hear from him, as was everyone in Hard Luck.

"They arrived twenty minutes ago," he said, and heard the relief in his own voice.

"How's Tracy?"

"They're examining her now, but she looks great for having spent the night in a snowbank. The hospital probably won't even need to admit her.

Abbey's own relief was audible. "And Duke?"

"Duke wasn't as fortunate," Sawyer replied. He leaned against the wall, able to relax now that he'd seen Duke. "Compound fracture of his arm, possible internal injuries—they haven't told him that part."

"How bad?"

"We don't know yet." He probably should've waited until he had all the details, but he'd wanted to call with the good news—Duke and Tracy were alive. Half of Hard Luck had stopped into the office at some point during the day, asking about the pair. Word of the crash had spread throughout the community.

"Will he be all right?" Abbey asked next.

"He's going in for surgery so the arm can be set. As for the other, it's too soon to tell. But my guess is Duke'll be as good as new in a few weeks."

"Thank heaven."

"Yes," Sawyer murmured.

"The others are with you?" Abbey asked.

"Yeah. They're waiting for me in the cafeteria."

As soon as he'd heard that the snowstorm had cleared over Fairbanks, Sawyer had headed for the airfield. It wouldn't take long to assemble the rescue team and go after the missing couple.

Before he'd made it to the plane, however, Ralph had come running over with the news that they'd been rescued. He, John, Ted and three of the others asked if they could accompany Sawyer. Nearly his entire crew had wanted to be at the hospital when Duke arrived.

Duke had friends. Damn good ones.

"I'll pass the word along," Abbey promised, sounding close to tears.

"Abbey, is everything all right?"

"Yes...yes, of course. It's just that I'm so relieved. Those two had me worried."

"You!" She'd been as cool as swamp grass with him. Knowing how the crash had affected him, she must have figured she needed to be strong. He'd married himself quite a woman, Sawyer thought, but then this wasn't the first time he'd recognized that.

TRACY WALKED into Duke's hospital room and experienced the sudden urge to cry. She'd waited what seemed like hours for him to be brought out of recovery.

His head was bandaged, his arm was in a cast, and an IV bottle steadily dripped fluid into a needle imbedded in the back of his hand. Dark circles shadowed his eyes.

He looked a mess.

The doctors had told her it would be some time before he woke, but she didn't care. They'd been through too much together for her to desert him now.

She sat down in the chair next to his bed, content to stay exactly where she was until he told her himself that he was all right. She didn't trust anyone else.

"Tracy?"

Sawyer O'Halloran walked into the room.

She gave him a weak smile. "That was one hell of an airplane ride," she teased.

He didn't smile. "I'll bet."

"You don't need to worry—I'm not going to sue."

He blinked in surprise. Obviously the thought had never occurred to him. But it probably had to others. After all, she *was* an attorney, they'd figure.

"How are you feeling?"

She smiled faintly. "Like I was in an airplane crash." The cut on her head was held together with a butterfly bandage, and she'd suffered a slight concussion, but her injuries weren't life-threatening. No frostbite, even.

She knew she looked a sight, but she didn't care. Nor was she willing to leave Duke's side until she knew for herself that he was going to pull through.

"Can I get you anything?"

"I'm fine, but thanks."

"I've booked a hotel room for you over at the Moose Suites," he said, and hesitated when she gave him an odd look. She couldn't help it. The Moose Suites?

"The place isn't as weird as it sounds. Clean rooms, reasonable rates. Ralph took your suitcase there." Sawyer handed her a room key.

"Thank you." Until he'd told her about the room, she hadn't given a moment's thought to where she'd stay. Once Duke awoke, she'd take a taxi to the hotel, shower and sleep for a week.

"I took the liberty of contacting your law firm."

Her gaze shot to him and she blinked. "Oh, my, I forgot about work." Neither her law practice nor her life outside this hospital room seemed quite real at the moment.

"I spoke with Mr. Nelson."

"He's the senior partner." Tracy bit her lower lip. She'd pushed the entire matter of her career and her life in Seattle out of her mind. She tried to picture her work calendar and remembered that she had a brief due Wednesday, a settlement hearing scheduled for Thursday, and on Friday— Oh, dear, there was something important on Friday, but for the life of her, she couldn't remember what it was.

"Mr. Nelson was sorry to hear about the accident. He sends his personal regards and asked me to tell you to take as long as you need."

"Thank you, Sawyer." For a woman as disciplined and organized as she was, it astonished Tracy that she could let something like her work commitments slip her mind.

"He asked if you'd give him a call when you were up to it."

"I . . . will." But not anytime soon, she thought.

"Until then," Sawyer continued, "you're not to worry. Mr. Nelson has everything covered."

She nodded, not knowing what to say. Her entire world centered in this small hospital room with the man who'd saved her life.

This was no exaggeration, no survivor's gratitude run amuck, but simple fact. Tracy had heard the men talking as they'd pulled Duke from the plane. They'd found the ruptured fuel line and said the pattern the plane made as it went down showed that Duke had purposely steered it so that his side of the aircraft received the greater impact.

Duke's skillful handling of the plane had saved their lives. Again and again Tracy heard the investigators' comments to that effect.

A nurse had told her she was lucky to be alive, and Tracy had quickly corrected her. Luck had nothing to do with it. She was alive because of Duke Porter, and she wasn't going to forget it.

"Do you need me for anything else?" Sawyer asked again.

"No..." She couldn't think, couldn't make sense of her incoherent impressions.

"Don't hesitate to phone if you or Duke need something," he instructed.

"I won't."

He handed her his business card, and for the first time Tracy realized she didn't have her purse. Sawyer appeared to understand without her having to say a word.

"Your purse is with your suitcase in the hotel room. It's locked away safe and sound."

As she thanked him, Sawyer moved to the other side of the hospital bed and studied Duke. "He's going to come out of all this just fine. Don't you worry."

Tracy nodded, closing her eyes as she mentally reviewed the list of his injuries. His arm wouldn't heal overnight. It'd be months before he regained full use of it. The cut on his head, which had required twenty-five stitches to close, had been even meaner and deeper than she'd realized. The physician who'd sewn it shut had complimented her on the resourceful way she'd wrapped it.

As for his internal injuries, it was too soon to tell the extent of the damage. At best, his vital organs had been shaken up a bit. At worst... Well, at worst was something she didn't want to even consider.

"I'm going to leave now," Sawyer told her.

She nodded.

"But I'll be back. Do you want me to bring you anything to eat?"

"Thanks, but no." The hospital had given her some warm broth, and she'd had tea and toast earlier. Food didn't appeal to her and probably wouldn't for some time.

"I shouldn't be gone more than a couple of hours."

"Okay."

Sawyer left the room.

Tracy scooted the chair as close to Duke's bed as she could. Because of the IV, she couldn't hold his hand, so she pressed her cheek against the side of the mattress and gently draped her fingers over his forearm.

She wasn't sure how much time had passed when she sensed that he was awake. Lifting her head, she noticed the way he ran his tongue over his lips, as if he was thirsty.

She stood and carefully poured ice water into a glass, adding a straw from a supply on the bedside table.

He rolled his head from side to side. "Tracy?"

"I'm here." She was inordinately pleased that hers was the first name he called.

His eyes fluttered open, and her heart filled with gratitude. She bent close to him. He raised his hand to her face and caressed her cheek.

Tracy battled the urge to weep and kissed the inside of his palm. "Sleep. Everything's wonderful. You're wonderful. I...am, too."

"Beautiful." The word rasped from his lips.

"Yeah, right." Tracy had no illusions about her looks. Especially now—she'd caught her reflection in the mirror.

She offered him the water and he sucked it greedily through the straw. The effort appeared to drain him, and he leaned back against the pillow and closed his eyes.

Content, Tracy sat down at his side and brushed the tears from her face.

BEN EXAMINED the dinner plate Bethany had carried up to his apartment. He grinned broadly when he lifted the lid and saw the hamburger bun. "Now this is more like it," he said, smiling up at her. He didn't know how many more of those healthy meals of hers he could stomach.

"Now listen, Ben, you've got to watch what you eat."

"I am, I am," he muttered. Not that he could avoid it, with Bethany standing guard over him every evening. He peeled back the bun and his heart sank with disappointment.

"What the hell is this?" he demanded. He noticed that his raised voice didn't intimidate her.

"It's a veggie burger."

"A *what?*"

"You heard me."

He groaned. Bethany had set out to starve him to death, and she was succeeding. His own flesh and blood, no less.

"Now, listen," he said disgustedly, "I've had more oat bran in the last three weeks than some horses."

"Ben—"

"You've shoveled more yogurt down me than any man should have to endure. I've put up with it, too, be-cause...because you mean well. But now I'm putting my foot down. Look at this," he said, pointing to his dinner plate. "You've ruined a perfectly good hamburger bun with this veggie . . . thing."

"Ben, you can't eat the way you used to. The least you can do is give this a taste. It's made with tofu and—"

"Tofu?" he cried, outraged. "Just what kind of man do you think I am? I hope to high heaven you didn't let anyone around here know your feeding me tofu!"

"No—"

"I had an egg for breakfast." He tossed that out, knowing she wasn't going to like it.

"Who's the executor of your estate?"

"Don't get smart with your elders," he barked.

"What about lunch?" she demanded, folding her arms and glaring at him. "Something tells me you didn't have the soup I set out."

"Hell, no. I cooked myself a pizza."

Bethany rolled her eyes. "I sincerely hope you've got your will made out. A pizza? Ben, really."

"I couldn't help it," he mumbled, feeling more than a little guilty. "Man does not live by bran alone." Although he had to admit he'd never been more regular— but he wasn't about to tell Bethany that. She might add even more to his diet.

"Just *try* the veggie burger."

Like he had much of a choice. Either he ate what she brought him or he waited until she left and made his way downstairs to rustle up some dinner. "All right," he said, but he could already tell he wasn't going to like it.

Bethany laughed unexpectedly. "I swear you're worse than a little kid. You'd think I'd brought you liver and onions."

"I like liver and onions." Now she was talking. Liver fried up in lots of bacon grease, not overcooked, either. He liked it tender, heaped with plenty of grilled onions. The thought of it set his mouth watering.

Bethany sat down across from him. "Remember, Mrs. McMurphy's coming for her interview tomorrow afternoon."

Ben wasn't likely to forget. The more he thought about letting a stranger into his kitchen, the more he was against the whole idea. He hadn't minded when Mariah worked for him, since she mostly stayed out of his way and let him cook. It'd been a luxury to have someone wait tables and collect dirty dishes.

But another cook! A woman, to boot. Not in his kitchen. Not while he lived and breathed. Well, it wouldn't take much to find fault with this cook Mitch and Bethany wanted him to meet.

"I talked with Mrs. McMurphy this afternoon," Bethany said. "She's excited to meet you."

"I'll just bet."

"She did a lot of the baking at the Sourdough Café and said she'd be willing to do that here, in addition to the other cooking."

"What'd she bake?" The way Ben figured, if he appeared interested and asked plenty of questions, Bethany might not realize he'd already made up his mind.

"Her specialty is strudel, although she said her cinnamon rolls were popular with the clientele."

Cinnamon rolls happened to be one of Ben's weaknesses. He never had gotten the hang of baking them himself. He liked his rolls made with plenty of real butter and drizzled with icing. His gaze dropped to the veggie burger, and he decided he'd gladly give a year's profits for a single bite of warm, butter-oozing cinnamon roll.

"All I want you to do is give Mrs. McMurphy a chance."

"Of course I will." Ben reached for the glass of milk and took a swallow, fearing she might read the insincerity in his eyes. The milk tasted terrible, and he spit it back into the glass.

"What'd you do to my milk?" he cried.

Bethany pinched her lips together. "I didn't do anything to it."

Ben held his glass up to the light. "It's . . . blue."

"It's nonfat."

If anything was going to kill him, it was this woman's attempt to manage his diet. "You can't spring a thing like nonfat milk on a man," he told her. "You should've warned me."

She folded her arms. "Don't you think you're overreacting just a tad?"

"Hell, no!" he cried. "A veggie burger, skim milk, and a bran muffin for dessert. If I didn't know better, I'd swear you were trying to kill me."

"Ben!"

"All right, all right." He sighed. "Thank you for bringing over my...dinner." To use the word loosely. He used to eat more than this for his midnight snacks.

"Now, what about your meeting with Mrs. McMurphy?"

She wasn't going to let up on this, Ben could tell. "I'll be cordial and treat her real nice." That was what Bethany wanted to hear, and he wasn't telling a lie. He'd be real cordial and polite when he showed her the door.

"Just to be on the safe side, I've asked Mrs. McMurphy to have dinner with Mitch and me following the interview," Bethany told him. "You're welcome to join us if you want."

Ben scowled. "It all depends on what you're cooking." Another night of veggie burgers, and he was likely to fade away to nothing.

DUKE AWOKE in the dim light and took several moments to update his memory. All he'd done for the better part of two days was sleep. Every time he opened his eyes, he discovered Tracy at his side. He wasn't disappointed this time, either. She'd curled up in the chair next to his bed and was sound asleep. Someone had covered her with a thin blanket.

At some point she must have showered and changed clothes, because she wore a sweater he couldn't remember seeing before. Having her at his side produced a warm feeling in the pit of his stomach. They'd been through a hell of a lot together. More than some people endured in a lifetime.

One thing was certain. Tracy was about the bravest woman he'd ever known. It couldn't have been easy for her, with him out of his mind with pain half the time.

He was proud of her, the way she'd figured out how to work the radio and contact Fairbanks. The way she'd looked after him. She was cool and capable, the kind of woman who always found a solution, no matter what the problem. A woman who wouldn't give up when times got tough.

She'd kissed him.

The memory had a dreamlike quality to it. When they'd heard the rescue chopper's approach, she been so excited that she'd kissed him. It didn't mean anything, Duke told himself. The kiss had been an expression of joy, of relief. Nothing more.

He'd tried over and over to remind himself of that, but it hadn't worked. As brief as the kiss had been, as meaningless as he attempted to convince himself it was, he'd enjoyed it.

If he'd been able, he'd have wrapped her in his arms and kissed her properly. His breath quickened just thinking about it. He'd take it slow and easy, draw her lower lip gently between his teeth, part her lips with his tongue and explore her mouth in a kiss neither one of them would soon forget. His heart began to pound wildly.

Duke forced himself to look away. This was Tracy Santiago he was fantasizing about. The woman he'd fought with time and time again. On closer examination, he understood that he'd always been attracted to her. Well, opposites were said to attract, he thought, and they'd proved it. He actually enjoyed their verbal battles, even looked forward to them. A few had gotten out of hand, but he was more to blame for that than she.

What he didn't like about Tracy, Duke realized, was the way he felt out of control whenever he was with her. It came to him then that he'd behaved around her the way Christian had acted around Mariah. All the while he'd been complaining about his secretary, he'd been falling in love with her.

Love. Could it be possible that he actually loved Tracy? The thought terrified him. He didn't want to feel this emotion, this . . . this vulnerability.

Dammit all, leave it to him to fall in love with some fancy, highfalutin Seattle attorney. A lot of good it would do either one of them.

Her life was in Seattle and his was in Hard Luck. Here it was, history repeating itself. His father had loved his mother enough to believe he could meld their worlds. In the end, they'd both been miserable.

Loving Tracy wasn't going to change a damn thing. He sure as hell wasn't going to give up his life and follow her into the city. As far as he was concerned, *Fairbanks* was overcrowded. He couldn't imagine what life would be like in a city the size of Seattle.

And as for her moving to Hard Luck, tempting though it sounded, Duke knew it wouldn't work. He couldn't ask a woman of Tracy's education and temperament to give up the bright lights for some dinky town in the Arctic.

That didn't leave much room for their relationship.

It wouldn't be easy to let her go, not when she was looking at him with stars in her eyes. He knew what she was thinking, because he'd had those same thoughts.

But it wouldn't work.

CHAPTER FIVE

TRACY STIRRED in the chair at Duke's bedside. She raised her arms high above her head and stretched, arching her back. Swallowing a yawn, she worked the stiff muscles of her shoulders. It took her a few moments to notice that Duke was awake. He was sitting up in bed watching her.

"Hello," she said, surprised at how shy she felt around him. "How are you feeling?"

"Better than I did a couple of days ago. How about you?"

"None the worse for wear." She untucked her legs from beneath her and stood. "Any idea how long I've been asleep?"

"Don't know. I've only been awake for half an hour or so myself. Actually I didn't expect to find you still here."

She saw the look of disapproval in his eyes and stopped herself from telling him she'd only left his side for brief periods since their rescue.

"Shouldn't you be back in Seattle?" Duke asked. "It's been what? Two, three days now?"

"The ... the senior law partner told me to take as long as I needed."

Duke's expression was grim. She could actually see him shutting her out; it was like a gate closing, blocking her passage. Now that they were safe, now that they were back, he seemed to be saying he wanted nothing to do with her.

"How much more do you need?" he asked. The words weren't harsh, but their message was—she didn't have to remain in Alaska on his account. In fact, he'd prefer it if she left.

"Nothing's holding you here, is it?"

"No," she admitted reluctantly, averting her gaze.

"You'll make your flight reservations then?" She glanced up, and his eyes burned into hers.

Her heart constricted, but she refused to let him know how deeply he'd wounded her. "I'll call the airlines at the first opportunity." Her hand trembled as she folded the blanket and set it on the small pillow she'd been using. Her lips trembled as she faced him again.

She'd never been as intimate with a man as she'd been with Duke, and she wasn't referring to anything physical. The closeness they'd shared was emotional. They'd touched each other's lives in ways that went beyond the mundane. Together they'd stared death in the eye, clinging to hope and to each other.

He wanted her to leave, but she couldn't, not without thanking him. The words that formed so easily in her heart, however, stuck in her throat.

"I won't say it's been fun," she said, making a feeble attempt at humor.

"That's one thing it hasn't been," he agreed.

She stood by his bedside and resisted the urge to brush the hair from his forehead. Often while he'd slept she'd felt free to touch him, to offer small gestures of tenderness. She knew he wouldn't welcome the informality now that he was awake.

Finally she managed to say, "Before I return to Seattle I want to thank you."

"Hey, you seem to forget I was the one who brought that plane down."

"No," she corrected, "the ruptured oil line was responsible for that. Your skill as a pilot is what saved us both." Then, because she felt it was important, she added, "I know what you did."

Even as she said the words she realized he would pretend ignorance and discount what the investigators had said. "You risked your own life to save mine."

"Nonsense."

Tracy hid a smile. She felt she knew Duke better than any man she'd ever dated.

"What's so damn funny?" he asked.

"You. I've talked to the men who investigated the crash site. They said that, from the evidence, you purposely put yourself at greater risk."

"Hogwash."

"Let's not argue," she said, knowing it would do no good to press the issue.

"Why not?" he asked, his eyes flashing with warmth and humor. "It's what you and I've done from the first. It feels right to clash wills with you. You're a worthy adversary."

She dipped her head, acknowledging the tribute. "I'll consider that a compliment."

His grin relaxed and he grew serious once more. "You did good, Santiago," he said, his gray eyes dark and intense. "It wasn't any picnic out there, but you were a real trooper."

"I couldn't have done it without you." There wasn't a single doubt about that.

"Sure you would've," he countered swiftly. "You've got mettle and spirit. I was out of it most of the time and—"

"Not all." He'd held her and reassured her, when he was the one who'd sustained the worst injuries. She'd never forget that. The fear would've destroyed her if it hadn't been for the solace she'd found in his arms.

"I'll admit you surprised me," Duke admitted. "A city girl like you."

She wanted to tell him she wasn't any different from Mariah or the other women who'd moved to Hard Luck in the past two years. Something in his eyes told her she'd be wasting her breath. In the past they'd taken delight in waging verbal battles—but the time for that was over. They'd progressed far beyond quarreling to a level of mutual respect. A week earlier she would have responded with indignation; now she let the matter drop.

"You'll go back soon then?" He made it sound like he couldn't be rid of her fast enough. Well, Duke never had been kind to her ego.

"Soon," she promised.

"If I ever happen to need an attorney," he said brightly, "I'll know who to call."

Of all the things he might have said, this affected her the most. She bit her trembling lower lip in an effort to stall the emotion that burned just beneath the surface.

"Hey, what'd I say?"

"Nothing." Laughing a little, she shook her head. "You're a hell of a man, Duke Porter. I never thought I'd say this, but I'm going to miss you like crazy." Her heart hammered with the pain of the coming separation.

"I never thought I'd miss you, either." His face was pinched, his eyes shadowed. This time she knew it wasn't due to his injuries. Parting was as difficult for him as it was for her. But Tracy sensed that he wasn't keen on her knowing it, so she pretended not to notice.

"Take some advice," Duke said, "and ditch Gavin. You deserve a real man."

Unfortunately the only one who fell into that category was here in front of her—and he was sending her away. "I'd already decided that."

His gaze held hers, then he asked, "A kiss for luck?"

She smiled and nodded. He held his good arm out to her, and she came into his embrace. She assumed he only meant to hug her, perhaps give her a peck on the cheek.

But Duke gathered her close and directed her lips to his. The kiss was like the man. He held back nothing, twining his fingers into her hair, slanting his mouth over hers in a breath-stealing kiss that rocked her senses. Her breath jammed in her lungs as her fingers dug into his shoulders.

She tasted his urgency, his hunger, experienced them herself. He wanted her and made no apologies.

Gradually, almost without her being aware, the kiss changed. Catching her lower lip between his teeth, he sucked gently, easing open her mouth enough to admit his tongue, awakening her own.

The kiss might have gone on even longer if not for a noise in the hallway outside the partially closed door.

Duke released her with a reluctance that should have thrilled her, but didn't. With little more than a kiss, he was sending her out of his life.

"Goodbye, Tracy. Godspeed."

"Godspeed," she returned in a choked whisper. And then, while she could still hold back the tears, she walked hurriedly from the room—and from his life.

BEN HAD HIS EXCUSES neatly arranged in his mind. He'd meet Mrs. McMurphy and they'd exchange pleasantries. Next, he'd read over her résumé and ask a number of appropriate questions. Enough for her to believe he was giving her serious consideration. When the interview was over, he'd announce that he needed a couple of days to decide and would get back to her by the end of the week.

That was the way situations like this were handled. Ben possessed enough business savvy to know how to give a job applicant the brush-off.

He'd make sure Mrs. McMurphy and Bethany didn't know what he had up his sleeve. That would be a mistake. Instead, he'd play along, let both women assume he was satisfied with the interview. Then he'd sit down and have dinner with Bethany and her family. Socialize with Mrs. McMurphy.

Ben would lay odds that Bethany wasn't serving any tofu burgers this evening. Not with company. He was dreaming of Southern fried chicken, potatoes mashed with real butter, and sour-cream gravy. Dreaming—that was all he'd be doing, knowing Bethany.

Mrs. McMurphy was due any moment, so Ben slowly made his way down the stairs. The café was empty and lifeless. Damn, but he missed the old hustle and bustle. In the past, he'd sometimes gone an hour or two without a customer, but that was different. This kind of silence was downright eerie.

The grill was stone cold, but if he closed his eyes, he could hear the hiss of bacon and hash-brown potatoes frying in the pan.

Anticipating the woman's arrival, Ben put on a small pot of decaffeinated coffee—Bethany would approve—and pulled out a chair. He made himself comfortable. As he sipped from his mug, he watched the Baron aircraft land. Sawyer was back—with the infamous Mrs. McMurphy.

Ben caught his first view of the cook and was surprised at how tall she was. She wore a long black wool coat and carried a wicker basket over her arm, like little Red Riding Hood come to visit the big bad wolf.

Sawyer was kind enough to escort her to the café personally. He stayed only long enough to check that Ben was downstairs.

"So you're Mrs. McMurphy," Ben said after Sawyer left. "Ben Hamilton." He extended his hand.

"I'm very pleased to make your acquaintance," the tall slender woman said.

Years earlier Ben had seen a plaque that said never to trust a skinny cook. He was apt to accept that advice.

"Come in and make yourself comfortable," he urged, motioning to the table where he'd been sitting. "May I take your coat?"

"Please." She slipped out of it; she wore a practical denim dress and boots. She put the basket down on the table and sat quickly, almost as if she feared her height would alarm him. Ben was a big man himself, well over six feet. It took more than a reed-thin woman to intimidate him.

"Could I get you a cup of coffee?" he asked, still playing politeness to the hilt.

"No, thank you."

She was prim, a bit shy, with friendly blue eyes that seemed to take up half her face. Her dark, gray-streaked hair was gathered in a loose bun at the nape of her neck. It was difficult to gauge her age; she could be anywhere between forty and sixty. Plain. No rings, he noted. No jewelry, for that matter.

Ben pulled out his chair and sat down himself.

"I've enclosed a number of letters of recommendation," she said, retrieving an envelope from her purse. Her hand shook slightly.

She was nervous, Ben realized, and found that downright puzzling. If he'd raised his voice, as he tended to do, he'd scare the poor thing out of ten years of her life.

He peeled open the envelope and took out three single sheets of paper. It wasn't until he started reading that he noticed the most enticing scent. A blend of apples and spices. It distracted him enough that he couldn't finish the letters.

He hesitated and glanced toward the wicker basket. His mouth watered. What was it Bethany had told him about Mrs. McMurphy's specialties? Oh, yeah—strudel and cinnamon rolls. Could it be possible . . . ?

His eyes were riveted on the basket.

"I brought along an apple strudel," Mrs. McMurphy said, following his gaze. "Mrs. Harris was kind enough to invite me for dinner this evening, and this was my way of thanking her."

"Did you bring anything else?" Bethany wouldn't hesitate to drag him before a firing squad for asking.

"Some cinnamon rolls," she said. "You're welcome to look over my résumé, of course, but I felt my rolls would speak for themselves. The recipe was my grandmother's."

"How thoughtful." Ben all but leapt from the table. He hadn't moved with this much agility for weeks.

Before a minute had passed he'd collected a fork and plate. His eyes feasted on the dish Mrs. McMurphy lifted from the basket.

Huge cinnamon rolls were piled high on the small platter. The frosting had melted over the top, just the way he liked.

"Please, Mr. Hamilton, help yourself."

Ben didn't require a second invitation. It demanded all his self-control not to dive in face first.

"I believe I'll have a taste," he said, as if he felt morally obligated to sample her wares since she'd gone to the trouble of bringing them.

He placed the largest one on the plate and licked the sweetness from his fingertips. This was heaven. Forget all that nonsense about bran and tofu.

Trying to disguise his absolute delight, he read over her résumé as he took the first bite.

"As I explained earlier, the recipe was my grandmother's. Although it's more expensive, I insist on using real butter." She mentioned this hesitantly, her eyes studying him.

Butter. She used real butter.

"I've tried margarines," Mrs. McMurphy said with regret, "but the rolls don't have the same richness or full-bodied flavor. If I come to work for you, Mr. Hamilton, I insist on using the best ingredients, and that means baking with butter."

Ben licked his fingers clean. "Of course."

"If you like, you could try another," she said, gesturing to the plate. "I brought plenty."

"Don't mind if I do." He had to rearrange the stack in order to get the larger of the remaining four.

"I suppose you'd like me to tell you a bit about my background," she said after a moment. Ben was far too busy eating to ask her questions.

"Please." He gestured for her to continue.

She listed a number of restaurants where she'd been employed in the past twenty years.

Ben barely listened. His eyes were half-closed in ecstasy as he chewed and swallowed.

"I understand there's a housing shortage in Hard Luck at present," Mrs. McMurphy said next.

Oh, yes, that was something he'd wanted to mention. A convenient excuse and, despite Bethany's interference, one he intended to use when he regretfully informed Mrs. McMurphy he wouldn't be able to hire her.

"I asked Mr. O'Halloran about the possibility of flying in from Fairbanks on a daily basis. Naturally it would depend on the hours you need me, and the flight schedule, but he seemed to think we could arrange something. Mrs. Harris also mentioned the lodge, and I called and spoke personally with Mr. Caldwell. They have a room I could rent during the week and then return to Fairbanks for the weekends."

Ben merely nodded and began to reach for a third roll.

"Perhaps you'd care to taste my strudel," Mrs. McMurphy suggested.

"Only if you insist." He shoved his empty plate toward her.

"I'm a widow," Mrs. McMurphy continued as she sliced off an ample portion of strudel and lifted it onto his plate. "My children are grown now, with lives of their own."

"Mrs. McMurphy—"

"Please, I'd be more comfortable if you called me Mary."

"All right—Mary," Ben said.

"The strudel is an old family recipe, as well," Mary said. "I don't think you'll be disappointed."

Ben slid a forkful into his mouth. If he'd been impressed with the cinnamon rolls, the apple strudel...well, the apple strudel was her triumph. The apples were tender and tart, and the delicate pastry seemed to dissolve on his tongue.

"Again, I use only real butter."

"Butter," he repeated, finishing the last exquisite bite.

"Yes. It's my one stipulation when it comes to baking. Seeing that you enjoy sweets, I wish I'd taken the time to bake a cheesecake."

"I prefer the strudel." The first piece was gone so quickly he hardly knew where it'd disappeared. He helped himself to a second serving, taking a thinner slice this time.

"I imagine you're wondering why I left the Sourdough Café after five years," Mary said. Ben felt a little—only a little—embarrassed that she had to conduct her own interview. After all, he was checking out her qualifications and couldn't ask questions at the moment. His mouth was full. "It broke my heart to leave," she explained, "but the café recently changed hands, and the new owner was looking to cut corners."

"I see." Mary McMurphy might be thin as a rail, but the woman knew her way around an oven. That much Ben would say for her. But there was far more to running a café than slapping together an apple strudel every now and then, he thought righteously.

It was as if the woman could read his mind. "In addition to the baking, I'm an excellent short-order cook. I can see from your menu that you offer hamburgers and so on. But I also have a number of specialties, including Southern fried chicken. People have been telling me for years that mine's as good as any colonel's."

"Fried chicken?"

"I hope you aren't partial to instant potatoes. Now, I realize that up here in the Arctic real potatoes might be hard to come by at times. I'm not nearly a stickler for this the way I am about using butter in my grandmother's recipes, but I do prefer to cook with real potatoes."

"Mashed with cream?"

"Does one mash them with anything else?" she asked, her large blue eyes wide and questioning.

"What about sour-cream gravy? Can you make that?" It was going to hurt like hell to tell this woman he wasn't going to be able to hire her.

"I've never made sour-cream gravy, but if you have a recipe, I'm sure I could learn."

"I have the recipe."

Mary McMurphy smiled at him. She placed the left-over strudel and cinnamon rolls back inside the wicker basket and draped the blue linen napkin over them.

"So it's not a problem to use butter?" She regarded him expectantly.

Before he could respond, the door opened and Bethany walked in.

"Butter?" he repeated. "I use it myself for all my baking."

"Wonderful!" Mary sounded genuinely pleased.

Slightly out of breath, Bethany approached the table. Ben knew she must have hurried away the minute school let out.

"Hello," Bethany greeted, her face wreathed in a welcoming smile. "You must be Mrs. McMurphy. I can't tell you how pleased I am to meet you."

"The pleasure's mine," the woman said with shy politeness.

"So," Bethany said, looking from Mary to Ben, "how'd the interview go?"

Ben eyed the basket, praying Bethany would never learn about his lapse.

"Very well," Mary supplied. "Ben's agreed to hire me, and furthermore he has no objection to my using butter in my recipes."

Hire her? Ben hadn't said one word about hiring her.

"Ben!" Bethany beamed with pleasure. "That's wonderful." She wrapped her arms around his neck and hugged him enthusiastically.

"I'll be able to start first thing Monday morning," Mary said, smiling broadly. "Now if you'll both excuse me a moment, I'll go freshen up."

As soon as she left, Bethany took a chair. "I'm really happy about this, Ben. Mrs. McMurphy's a dear, isn't she?" She paused. "You'll have to forgive me for doubting you, Ben. I was so sure you were going to find some flimsy excuse why you couldn't hire her. I was prepared to wage war with you. I left the school with my cannons loaded," she said, laughing lightly. "And to think it was all for naught."

TRACY SAT STARING out her office window. Located on the top floor of a Seattle high rise, it had a view that was the envy of everyone who saw it. Puget Sound stretched out before her in all its splendor—deep blue water, islands thick with green firs, sailboats with bright billowing sails. A ferry sounded its horn as it pulled away from the pier headed for Bainbridge Island.

October, as always, had brought warm Chinook winds, and while it was already winter in Hard Luck, Seattle was enjoying a lingering summer.

She'd been back a week, but it seemed more like a year. What had once been so familiar now felt strange and...a little pointless. Every night she hurried home, waiting for some word from Duke. A letter, a postcard, a message on her answering machine. She knew better than to hope, but she couldn't seem to make herself stop.

The only evidence of the sixteen hours she'd spent trapped in the downed plane was a thin red line on the left side of her forehead. And a heart that hungered for her pilot....

She could have disguised the scar with makeup, but didn't. It was like a badge of honor. A souvenir of those hours alone with Duke. Unfortunately her heart wouldn't heal as easily as her skin had.

She couldn't think of him and not get choked up. A friend, a fellow attorney, had taken her to lunch earlier that day and suggested Tracy talk to a counselor. Janice seemed to think that because Tracy wasn't interested in talking about the experience at every opportunity, she might require a professional to help her deal with the ordeal.

Talk about it. That was all Tracy had done for days on end. She was sick of the subject. She'd told the story countless times, answered a million questions. What more did people expect of her?

True, she'd been vague about some of the details, but those details weren't meant to be shared. What had happened between her and Duke was special, and it belonged only to them.

She wondered if he'd been hounded with questions from his friends and what he'd told them about the time they'd shared.

Tracy had assumed, hoped really, that once she was back to her normal life, she wouldn't think about Duke as much. It hadn't happened. He was with her night and day. With every waking thought. Every nonwaking one, too.

He often visited her dreams and she awoke feeling warm and happy, remembering the night she'd spent in his embrace. But the happiness never lasted. Maybe Janice was right. Maybe she did need to see a counselor.

It probably wasn't mentally sound to prefer a life-threatening plane crash to waking up safe in her own bed.

Filled with nervous energy, Tracy circled her desk. She picked up one of the greeting cards she'd bought that afternoon while walking along the waterfront. Some were humorous. Some sincere. Others blank. But they all had one thing in common.

They were meant for Duke.

The temptation to mail him one, just one, was almost too strong to resist. It'd be nothing more than a friendly gesture to ask how he was, how his arm was healing. Or so she told herself. Still, she hesitated.

Duke wasn't like any man she'd ever known. What applied to other relationships didn't work with him. Always before, Tracy had been the one in charge of a romantic association. She decided when they'd date. Where they'd go, and most importantly, how often they'd see each other. This time, Tracy couldn't set the rules, though. Duke was a man who followed his *own* rules.

The intercom buzzed. Tracy walked around her desk and leaned over to push the button. The receptionist's voice came on. The office was technically closed, and it was late to be receiving phone calls.

"Yes, Gloria?"

"I'm sorry to disturb you, Ms. Santiago. I was late putting on the answering service and the call came through. I can ask the caller to try you again tomorrow if you want."

"Who is it?"

"All I know is that the person's a friend of yours from Hard Luck."

Tracy literally fell into her chair. "Put him through." Her heart felt as if it was going to leap right out of her chest with happiness.

Duke.

"This is Tracy Santiago," she said doing her best to sound nonchalant.

"Tracy, it's Mariah. Christian and I got back last night, and we just heard the news. How are you? It was such a shock to learn you and Duke were in a crash."

"I'm fine." Hiding her disappointment was more than she could manage.

"You don't sound so fine."

"I am, really."

"Christian and I leave for two weeks and it's like the whole world goes crazy while we're away. It must have been *terrible* for you."

"No," Tracy answered honestly. "It wasn't so bad." Then, because she needed to know, she asked, "Have you talked to Duke lately?"

"Oh, yes, right away, as soon as we heard about the accident."

"How is he?" Tracy had to know.

"He looks good."

"His arm?" she asked anxiously. "Is it bothering him?"

"Not that he mentioned."

But then, Duke wasn't the type to complain. What she wanted, Tracy decided, was to hear Mariah tell her that Duke was pining away for want of her. But that would have been far too much to expect.

"How was the honeymoon?" Tracy asked, needing to change the subject.

"Oh, Tracy, I'm so in love!"

"Christian's a good man," Tracy murmured.

"I wasn't talking about him." Mariah giggled. "I mean I'm crazy about cruising." Then she grew serious.

"We had a marvelous time, and I'm more in love with my husband than ever."

Tracy wasn't surprised; those two were made for each other. Gathering her nerve, she said, "Listen, I need to get off the phone. The next time you see Duke tell him I said hello, will you?"

"Sure." But Mariah sounded hesitant.

"You won't be seeing him?"

"Of course I will. He works with Christian, after all. He's grounded, you know, because of his arm."

Tracy had suspected he wouldn't be able to fly and knew that was probably the most difficult aspect of his recovery. Duke was more comfortable in the air than on land.

"He's been sort of a grouch lately," Mariah said hesitantly.

That was understandable.

"If anyone asks him about the accident, he bites off their heads. I was in the office when Bill Landgrin made the mistake of mentioning how difficult it must have been for the two of you to be trapped in the plane together. Bill said something along the lines of you being a, uh, man hater."

Tracy didn't hate men, although she'd been accused of it before. In fact, if she recalled correctly, it was Duke who'd made the accusation.

"Bill certainly didn't mean anything by it," Mariah elaborated. "Everyone knows you and Duke have never gotten along. Neither one of you has made a secret of your feelings."

"True."

"Well, Duke went ballistic. Christian told me Duke shoved Bill up against the wall—and remember, he's only got one good arm."

"They...fought?"

"No, Christian broke it up."

"Good." Duke was in no condition to fight, especially with his left arm in a cast.

"But Sawyer and Christian talked it over and suggested maybe it would be better if Duke took some time off. He's not getting along with anyone right now."

Tracy's inclination was to defend him. Duke had been through a far rougher ordeal than she had. If ever he needed his friends, it was now.

"The next time you see him," Tracy said, chewing her lower lip, "tell him..." She didn't know what to say, or even if he wanted to hear from her. Dejected, she continued, "Tell him I said hello and...and that I hope he's feeling better."

"Sure thing," Mariah promised. "Take care, okay?"

"I will," Tracy promised, and replaced the receiver. She eyed the greeting cards on her desk and sorted through them, trying to decide which one she would mail Duke.

CHAPTER SIX

FROM THE SOUNDS below, it seemed every available chair in the Hard Luck Café was filled. Nevertheless, Ben frowned. If he fired Mary McMurphy, he couldn't very well claim it was because business was slow. She'd been with him for several days now and had won more hearts than a beauty queen.

Ben swore every man in town had gained five pounds on Mary's cinnamon rolls. She baked a fresh batch every morning. He had it on good authority that his customers formed a line outside the café the minute she pulled them from the oven. The aroma wafted through the cold morning air like nerve gas, attacking anyone within striking distance.

The café had done more business in the week since he'd hired Mary than in any seven-day period since he'd owned the place.

Ben had no cause for complaint—but truth was, her popularity was a bit irksome. Soon folks would forget all about him. His biggest fear was that his long-time customers would prefer Mary's cooking to his own.

She'd proved to be so popular with his customers that he'd catch hell if he laid her off now. He felt thwarted at every turn.

So he sat in his apartment above the kitchen and stewed.

Because he was still officially recovering from his heart surgery, he wasn't allowed to do any of the cooking yet. Nevertheless it drove him crazy to hear all the commotion going on below. In his very own café.

The noise gradually died down, but it would take more than dollar signs to sweeten his sour mood. How quickly he'd been forgotten. All his customers really cared about were their stomachs, he decided.

"Mr. Hamilton," Mary called from the foot of the stairs.

Ben ignored her.

"Mr. Hamilton," she tried again, her voice closer this time. She marched up to the top of the stairs and waited. Ben sat in his recliner, pretending to be asleep.

"I hope I'm not disturbing your rest," she said, despite his closed eyes. "There seems to be a lull, and I thought I'd bring you up a cup of coffee and the last cinnamon roll."

Ben's eyes snapped open. She'd brought him a cinnamon roll?

"I know Bethany's worried about your fat intake, and I don't blame her, but if you watch what you eat the rest of the day, I don't think one little goodie would hurt you."

Ben couldn't agree more. It'd been hell smelling those rolls day in and day out and not being able to taste one.

"I'll make sure everything in your diet balances out myself," Mary told him as she set the mug and plate on the small table next to the recliner.

"I was hoping you'd come down this morning," she said hesitantly.

He grumbled a nonreply. No one wanted him around, not with Mary and her cinnamon rolls and strudels to satisfy them.

"Everyone's asking about you," she added.

Ben doubted that.

"I'm not nearly the conversationalist you are," she stated matter-of-factly. "The men miss talking to you. It's different having a woman there, they tell me."

Ben brightened somewhat. So his friends hadn't completely abandoned him. That was encouraging.

"Another thing," Mary said shyly. "I can't quite seem to make the sourdough hotcakes the right consistency. The customers like my rolls well enough for now, but they're going to get tired of those soon. Then they'll want their sourdough hotcakes, and I'm afraid I'm going to disappoint them."

So maybe the woman wasn't the paragon everyone assumed. "You'll learn," he assured her, feeling generous.

He sampled the roll and was reminded anew why his customers willingly stood in the cold waiting for the café to open each morning. But Mary was right about her pastries being a novelty that would soon wear off, he thought smugly. She'd sell plenty, but there'd be a need for his hotcakes, same as always, within a week or two.

Mary lingered, nervously shifting her weight from foot to foot. "If it wouldn't be too much trouble, I thought I'd go over the dinner menus with you."

"Sure. Now's as good a time as any." He motioned for her to sit. He couldn't very well keep her standing while he remained in his recliner.

"It won't take long, I promise."

"No problem," he muttered, and because it was true, he added, "I don't have anything better to do."

"I found a large prime rib in the freezer," Mary said, glancing over at him. "Were you saving it for something special? If not, I'd like to put it on the menu for Friday night."

"There's probably several in there. Sure, go ahead."

"Do you have any particular way of cooking your prime rib?" she asked, deferring to him once more.

The last time he'd made one had been at least three months ago. "I slow-cook the roast in a bed of salt. Takes a few hours, but it's worth it."

"My, that sounds wonderful," Mary said, scribbling notes on her pad.

"I've got the recipe tucked away in the kitchen. Somewhere. If you like, I'll get it for you." He just hoped he could find it before Friday.

"That would be perfect." Her face glowed when she smiled. "If the rib is as good as you say, you might consider making the prime rib a regular Friday-night special."

"We might," he said, but he was unwilling to commit himself to it. In the past he'd saved those rib roasts for special occasions such as Founder's Day—commemorating the July arrival of Adam O'Halloran in 1931—and other important dates like Christmas and Easter. He hadn't thought about making a weekly special out of it. She might be on to something.

"I should've started with Monday's dinner, instead of Friday's, shouldn't I?" Mary continued, raising a hand to tuck a few wisps of hair behind her ear. Several appeared to have escaped her bun. Ben found her nervousness rather endearing.

"What's for dinner this evening?" he asked, pulling his attention back to the matters at hand.

"Shrimp linguine with lemon sauce," she said, and glanced hesitantly at him. "If that suits you?"

Actually it sounded great. With all his cooking experience, Ben had never gotten the hang of preparing shellfish. He made a fairly decent shrimp Creole, but that was about it.

"I think you'll like the linguine," Mary said, "and I promise you won't even suspect it's low-fat."

Ben frowned; he sure hoped Mrs. McMurphy hadn't turned into another Bethany. He didn't know if he could stomach any more veggie burgers.

"I promise you'll never guess," she repeated, offering him a bright smile. He noticed that her back stiffened at his skeptical look. "I'm a woman of my word, Mr. Hamilton. If you find the linguine unsatisfactory, I'll cook you the meal of your choice. Agreed?"

He didn't hesitate, because he knew what he wanted. A cheeseburger. It'd been weeks, no, months, since he'd last sunk his teeth into a good old-fashioned burger. "Agreed."

Mary proved to be a woman of her word. Ben ate two helpings of shrimp linguine and would've asked for more, but she ran out. It seemed the dish was as popular with his customers as it was with him.

Midmorning the following day, Ben drifted down the stairs. It was the first time he'd made the trip when Mary was actually cooking in his kitchen. She must have heard him, because she turned around, spoon in hand. When she saw it was Ben, she smiled broadly.

"Why, Mr. Hamilton, this is a pleasant surprise."

He grumbled something about being bored. He noticed several cookbooks spread out across the counter and wondered what she was doing now. No cook he'd ever known cooked from a book, except on rare occasions.

"You couldn't have come at a more opportune time," she said. "Would you mind taste-testing something for me?"

He couldn't think of a reason to refuse, and his breakfast of yogurt and fresh fruit had worn off long ago. "I suppose."

The next thing he knew, he was sitting at the counter. Soon Mary appeared with a filled hamburger bun divided into fourths. She wore an apprehensive look. "I'm having my first taste of this, as well."

"Hamburger?"

"No... this is something different."

He let Mary try hers first, watching as she took a bite. Her face remained expressionless for several seconds, then she smiled and nodded. "This isn't bad."

"What is it?" Ben felt a man had a right to know what he was tasting.

"Just try it," she urged.

He would've refused if he wasn't so damn hungry. He bit tentatively into the bun. He wasn't exactly sure what was in the filling, but whatever it was tasted exotic. In fact, it was downright flavorful.

"Not bad," he agreed. "What is it?"

Mary McMurphy's smile stretched from ear to ear. "A veggie burger. I combined several recipes and added a few ingredients of my own."

Ben wouldn't have believed anyone could make vegetables appetizing enough to serve on a hamburger bun, but she'd done it. He polished off the first quarter and reached for the second.

"Do you like it?" she asked eagerly.

He probably should've played it cool, let her think the food was just passable, but her eyes were so wide and hopeful. For the life of him, Ben couldn't dash her spirits. "It's good enough to eat, which is more than I can say about Bethany's. That stuff could kill a man's appetite for years to come."

Happiness radiated from her smile. "Thank you, Ben."

To the best of his knowledge, this was the first time Mary McMurphy had called him anything other than Mr. Hamilton.

DUKE STOPPED and checked his mailbox at the Hard Luck post office once a week or so. He rarely received more than bills. Occasionally he got a letter from his mother, but that happened only a few times a year.

He unlocked Box E and retrieved one envelope. The first thing he noticed was the handwriting. Not a bill; his bills were computer-generated. As soon as he saw the return address—in Seattle—he knew the letter was from Tracy.

He resisted the temptation to rip open the envelope then and there. Back at the bunk house, he sat on the end of his bed and tugged open the flap. Inside was a business card, with her name scrawled across the front in bold letters, and a greeting card, with a note inside. He read it eagerly:

Hello Duke,
Just a note to check up on my knight in shining armor. How's the arm doing?
I'm back into the swing of matters here, busy as ever.
You mentioned that if you were ever in need of an attorney, you'd call on me. I hope you meant that. I've taken the liberty of enclosing my business card. Mariah said you'd had a run-in with Bill Landgrin.

I hate all the questions, too. I still think of you.

Fondly,
Tracy Santiago

Fondly. What the hell did that mean? *I still think of you.* What was she saying? Duke read the card a second time and then a third. He scowled, wondering exactly what Mariah had told her about his clash with Bill. He hoped she didn't know how angry and aggressive he'd been, how much he'd overreacted. Losing control was out of character for him. Granted, Landgrin was a jerk, but a verbal putdown or two would've put him in his place. No, Duke had lashed out for only one reason—he missed Tracy.

For days now he'd been fighting memories of her. And losing the fight. This kind of weakness was foreign to Duke, but he was beginning to realize he couldn't ignore the effect she'd had on his heart. Even his mind was playing tricks on him. Thoughts of her invaded his sleep. Night after night, she was there to greet him when he closed his eyes.

He missed her. He missed her smile and the way the corners of her mouth turned up ever so slightly, as if she didn't want him to see how amused she was. He missed her sarcasm and her opinionated ideas. He even missed their verbal battles, although he was no longer interested in finding fault with her, the way he'd been in the past.

Reading the card she'd sent intensified the feeling of emptiness a hundredfold.

The amount of time he spent thinking about Tracy contradicted all his beliefs about personal discipline. He couldn't *stop* thinking about her. He wondered if she'd taken his advice and broken off her relationship with that "sensitive" character she'd been dating. He wondered if she lay awake at nights remembering the kiss they'd shared. Damn, but that woman packed a wallop.

Unsure of how to respond to Tracy's card, Duke tucked it inside his locker. Because he needed to think, he wandered over to the Hard Luck Café for a cup of coffee.

Ben Hamilton was up and around a little more these days, and if Duke was lucky, he might find Ben alone. He wanted a chance to talk with him for a few minutes. Privately.

Ralph and Ted were sitting at the counter when Duke walked in. He hadn't expected to find his fellow pilots lingering over coffee this late in the morning. It was quite obvious that they weren't any happier to see him than he was to run into them.

"Duke, good to see you," Ben greeted him. At least one person in Hard Luck hadn't turned traitor. "How's the arm?"

"Don't ask," Ralph advised the cook. "He's liable to chew your head off."

Duke didn't take the bait. While it might be true that he'd been a bit short-tempered lately, he didn't think his friends should hold it against him. He was a pilot, after all, and any pilot would react badly to being grounded.

"How about coffee and a cinnamon roll?" Ben invited.

"Sure thing," Duke said, purposely sitting several seats down from the other men.

Ben brought over the coffee and pastry, and Duke glanced toward the men he'd once considered his friends. In retrospect, though, he didn't blame them. He *had* been in a foul mood since his release from the hospital. His inability to fly wasn't their fault—and it wasn't the only reason for his bad temper. If he was looking for something—or someone—to blame, it would be Tracy.

"I imagine you're feeling . . . restless these days," Ben said, leaning casually against the counter.

"Yeah, you could say Duke's restless," Ralph muttered, his elbows propped on the counter while he held his mug with both hands. His eyes seemed riveted straight ahead.

Duke's jaw tightened. He and Ralph had argued just the other morning; Duke really couldn't remember why. Over something trivial, no doubt.

He wasn't accustomed to having this much free time. He'd thought he could work in the office during his downtime, but all he seemed to do was get in the way. Mariah's replacement had been trained, and everything was under control there. Sawyer took pity on him, now and then offering him some menial administrative task. On a good day he could count on killing an hour, maybe two, in the Midnight Sons office.

The rest of the time he was on his own. He'd read more books in the past couple of weeks than in the entire previous year. Television didn't hold his attention; never had. So he'd been reduced to playing solitaire. He'd played for hours yesterday—then realized he was a card short.

That was what his argument with Ralph had been about, he recalled. Ralph had lent him the deck, and Duke had accused his friend of knowingly holding back that one card. Okay, so maybe he'd overreacted.

Duke remembered how Ralph and the other pilots had risked their own safety to search for his downed plane, and he felt an immediate surge of regret. Next time he was in Fairbanks, he'd pick up a new deck of playing cards for Ralph. No need to say anything; his friend would get the message.

"I hope this ornery cuss doesn't give you a hard time, Ben," Ted said as they paid their tab.

Again Duke held his tongue. He waited until the two pilots had left the café, then forcefully expelled his breath.

"So you've been a bit out of sorts lately," Ben said, pulling up a stool and sitting on the opposite side of the counter.

"Maybe," was all Duke would admit. "I've got too much damn time on my hands."

"Know what you mean," Ben replied. "You're talking to a man who's spent the last month twiddling his thumbs. All I got to say is it's no wonder our country has problems, with daytime TV as bad as it is."

Even knowing that Ben was half-serious, Duke couldn't keep from laughing. He was still chuckling when the door opened and Sawyer strolled inside.

"Howdy, Ben," Sawyer said, sliding onto the stool next to Duke. "How's it going, Duke?"

Although he would've preferred a few more minutes alone with Ben, Duke smiled. Shrugging, he said, "Oh, not bad, considering."

"Where's Mrs. McMurphy?" Sawyer asked next.

Duke had been wondering the same thing.

"She decided to organize the storeroom," Ben explained. "I've been meaning to do that myself, but I kept putting it off. I feel guilty letting her do it by herself, but she insisted. I did make her promise to call me if she had any problems."

"Leave it to a woman to get a person organized," Sawyer said, with a year's worth of marriage behind him. "Abbey and I hadn't been married a month before she emptied every closet in the house. She found a few things that turned out to be worth a pretty penny, too.''

"Like what?" Ben asked.

"A couple of old baseball cards I had as a kid. I gave them to Scott for his birthday, and you'd think I'd handed the boy a piece of gold. He loved them.''

"Trust me, the only thing Mary's going to find in that storeroom has long expired," Ben said. He looked at Christian. "What's Mariah up to these days?"

"Organizing," he said with a wide grin, "what else? She's getting the house set up, but that shouldn't take long. Last I heard, she was talking to Matt and Karen about capitalizing on the tourist business.''

Duke sipped his coffee. Who would've believed women would have such a strong impact on the community? From the first, he'd known there'd be changes when the women arrived, but he hadn't been sure they'd be *positive* changes. Now he had to acknowledge that they were.

"I imagine you're getting fidgety," Sawyer said to Duke.

That had to be the understatement of the century. "A little.''

"Personally I don't know what you're doing hanging around Hard Luck for," Ben said.

"He's right," Sawyer tossed in. "You've accumulated plenty of sick leave, plus your vacation time. Why don't you do some traveling, take a break?"

"And just exactly where do you suggest I go?" Duke asked.

Ben and Sawyer remained silent.

"Any ideas of where I should take this vacation?" he asked a second time.

"Yeah," Sawyer said slowly.

"I have a suggestion or two," Ben added.

"I'm all ears."

"Seattle," both Ben and Sawyer said at the same moment.

The two men stared at each other, then laughed uproariously. They were still laughing as Duke hurried out.

AS SHE SORTED through the morning's mail, Tracy noticed there was nothing from Duke. By her best estimate, he'd received her greeting card a week earlier. In that time she hadn't heard a thing from him. Tracy sighed; she'd been a fool to send the card. He'd made it plain when she left that he didn't want anything more to do with her.

Determinedly she pulled her gaze away from her desk calendar. With a court case coming to trial—and jury selection that morning—she had far more important subjects to occupy her mind.

She checked her watch and realized she was due in court in less than twenty minutes. She was never late, especially for court.

Just as she was about to place her file folder in her briefcase, her secretary, Gloria, buzzed her on the office intercom. "There's a call for you on line one."

"I don't have time for it now. I've got to get over to the courthouse," she said. "Would you take a message, Gloria?" This case was an important one, and Tracy had mulled long and hard over the best way to approach the jury.

"I'll get Mr. Porter's number and—"

Tracy dropped her file. "I'll take the call," she said. She closed her eyes and drew a deep breath before she reached for the telephone receiver. "This is Tracy Santiago."

"Hello, Tracy."

He sounded wonderful, vibrant, healthy. Close. As if he was in the room next door, instead of several thousand miles north.

"Duke." She kept her eyes fixed on the small Waterford crystal clock on the corner of her desk. "It's *so* good to hear from you." She knew she sounded thrilled; it didn't matter. She couldn't hide her feelings from him, and she wasn't even going to try.

"I thought I'd give you a call to thank you for the card."

"My pleasure. Listen, Duke, I really am pleased to hear from you. I don't want you to think I'm giving you the brush-off, but I have to be in court in a few minutes. If you'll give me your phone number, I'll call you back the minute I'm free."

He hesitated.

"Duke? Your phone number?"

"I've always been taught that the man should call the woman."

She groaned out loud. "I don't have time to debate protocol. Just give me your phone number."

"I'll call you. Now hurry up or you'll be late."

"Duke, you're being unreasonable!"

He chuckled. "Give 'em hell, sweetheart."

Before she could respond, the line went dead.

"Duke," she cried in frustration. *Weeks,* she'd waited weeks to hear the sound of his voice, and now she *still* had to wait. And all because of some archaic rule he'd learned as a boy!

Well, she didn't have time to worry about it now. Grabbing her briefcase, she hurried out the door. When she returned, though, she'd move heaven and earth to find that man's phone number.

DUKE SAT ON THE BED in the fancy Seattle hotel room and sighed. He'd come a hell of a long way, and even now he wasn't sure he'd done the right thing.

Oh, he'd found plenty of reasons to visit Seattle. None of which had anything to do with Tracy. But he wasn't going to kid himself.

The purpose of this trip wasn't to take a vacation. It wasn't even to look over house plans or arrange for building materials to be shipped to Hard Luck. It didn't have to do with the list of plane parts Sawyer had asked him to check into, either.

The reason he was sitting on a bed costing him a hundred and fifty bucks a night was Tracy Santiago. He'd come to see her because he hadn't been able to stay away.

"Court," Duke repeated. She was a career woman, he reminded himself. She wasn't going to drop everything in her life because he was in town for a few days. Hell, she didn't even *know* he was in town. He hadn't gotten around to telling her he was in Seattle. She'd find out soon enough.

But he wasn't staying long. Not at these prices.

He walked over to the desk and picked up the room-service menu. One glance assured him he'd prefer to dine out.

Tucking the room key securely in his pocket, he left the hotel and walked onto the street outside. More people occupied the sidewalk in this one square block of Seattle than walked through Hard Luck in a year.

All the activity made Duke nervous. He didn't know how people could ever get used to this kind of racket. Cars, buses, horns and sirens...

The noise level didn't improve as Duke walked down-hill toward the Seattle waterfront and Pike Place Market. If anything, it got worse. Even Anchorage wasn't this crowded.

Realizing he was hungry, Duke waited in line for ten minutes to order some fish and chips from one of the stands that dotted the piers. The deep-fried fish was tasty, and he enjoyed it so much he got back in line to buy a second order.

As he ate he gazed around him. The snow-capped mountaintops of the Olympics showed in the distance. The scenery was very nice, he observed, but nothing he couldn't see in his own state.

When he passed the aquarium, he decided to go in. It was well worth the fee, and he wandered around there for an hour or so. He figured that should be enough time for Tracy to finish at court and be back in her office.

He pulled out her business card, found Fourth Avenue on his map and walked down the street until he located her building.

He stood across the street and counted the floors until he found the twenty-first. He wondered if she had an office with a window and suspected she did. She wasn't a partner yet, but he didn't doubt she'd become one in time. She was ambitious and dedicated.

He felt a sense of pride—and a kind of fear. Their lives, their careers, couldn't possibly coexist. There was no common ground. Except...love? But love, no matter how strong, wasn't enough to wipe out the differences. Damn, he wanted to see her, though.

The fact that he happened to spot her on the crowded Seattle sidewalks could be nothing less than fate. All at once she was on the other side of the street, walking at a clipped pace, presumably back from her lunch break. Checking his watch, he saw that it was almost one. She must be heading over to the courthouse. Her briefcase was in her hand and her steps were filled with purpose.

"Tracy," he shouted, but she didn't hear.

He tried again, racing down the sidewalk.

She paused and glanced over her shoulder, not realizing he was on the other side of the street.

She looked good. Real good. Her hair bounced ever so slightly as she walked. He'd forgotten what a beautiful woman she was. He must have been blind earlier. Long shapely legs, a tiny waist and hips that looked—

He walked straight into a little old lady who glared at him as if she was certain she recognized his picture from a post-office "wanted" poster.

"I beg your pardon, ma'am."

"You might look where you're walking, young man," she scolded.

"I do hope you'll forgive me," he said, but his gaze followed Tracy. She was racing up a flight of steps into the King County Courthouse.

"Don't let it happen again," the woman said.

"I won't," Duke promised, sidling over to the curb. He looked both ways, then quickly jogged across the street. A horn blared a warning, which he ignored.

"Tracy!" He tried calling her again, hurrying into the building just as she stepped into an empty elevator. Because he had to walk through the metal detector, he missed it and was forced to wait. Not knowing which floor she was headed for, he waited until her elevator stopped and noted it was the fifth.

As soon as the next elevator returned to the lobby, he stepped inside and pushed the button for five.

The fifth-floor hallway seemed even busier than the street. Duke edged his way into the courtroom and looked around. Apparently this was a high-interest case, judging by the media coverage.

Duke slipped into a row near the back and sat down.

Within a couple of minutes, the bailiff instructed everyone in the courtroom to rise. The judge, dressed in flowing black robes, stepped into the room and took his position. The jury was already seated.

"Are you ready for your opening statement now, Ms. Santiago?" Judge Kingsley asked Tracy.

She stood. "Yes, Your Honor, I am."

Duke strained to see her client. He appeared to be a man in his thirties, perhaps younger. For no reason he cared to examine, Duke experienced a twinge of jealousy. No doubt Tracy was a popular attorney. She was sharp, decisive, thorough. And beautiful. What jury could refuse her? If he was the prosecutor, Duke knew he'd be worried.

Tracy stood slowly and walked toward the jury box. She smiled at the twelve men and woman, her pose relaxed.

"Ladies and gentlemen," she began confidently, "I'm here today to prove to you beyond a shadow of a doubt that my client is not guilty. As this case unfolds, you will be assured that Jack Makepeace acted purely in self-defense. He—"

She turned and faced the courtroom, and by some fluke her gaze landed on Duke.

She stopped, and faltered slightly.

Her arms dropped. Her eyes widened. Duke could see the muscles work in her throat.

"Ms. Santiago," the judge asked, "are you all right?"

She walked over to the table and poured herself a glass

of water. "I'm fine, Your Honor," she said, glaring at Duke.

Maybe she wasn't as pleased to see him as he'd hoped.

CHAPTER SEVEN

TRACY TOOK another swallow of water and waited for her heart to stop pounding. *Duke was in Seattle.* A small matter he hadn't bothered to disclose when they spoke earlier.

She looked at him a second time and frowned openly, letting him know she was furious. How dared he do this to her in the middle of her opening statement?

"Ms. Santiago, is there a problem?" the judge asked a little impatiently.

"I beg the court's indulgence," Tracy said. "I... needed a sip of water." She made an effort to compose herself and walked toward the jury box, hoping the twelve men and women were more forgiving than the judge.

By sheer force of will and years of practice, Tracy was able to finish her presentation without further incident. She dared not look at the court observers again, for fear Duke would distract her. Nevertheless, she was aware of his scrutiny as she spoke. She could almost hear him tell her to "give 'em hell." She might have, too, if she hadn't been so shaken by his unexpected appearance. As it was, she feared she hadn't made any substantial progress in proving her client's innocence.

When the trial recessed at four, Tracy spoke briefly with her client, then reeled around to confront Duke. The minute they were alone, she fully intended to give *him* hell.

He was gone.

Had he been a figment of her overactive imagination? Perhaps the phone call had been responsible for making her think she'd seen him when she hadn't. Maybe, just maybe, she was losing whatever sanity she still possessed.

Taking her briefcase with her, she headed out of the courtroom and back to her office. The minute she got there, she'd phone Hard Luck to get the name of his hotel. She was in the hallway walking toward the elevator when she saw him leaning indolently against the wall. He flashed her an easy smile.

The color remained high in Tracy's cheeks, and she scowled at him with the full force of her annoyance, which by this time was considerable. But despite her outrage, simmering just below the surface, was joy. Absolute joy.

"You might have told me you were in Seattle," she snapped, not knowing which emotion to express first.

"You were on your way to court," he reminded her.

"But you might have said *something*," she returned.

He looked good. Better than good. Healthy and vital. Whole. His left arm, cast and all, was supported by a sling, but it didn't distract from his strong masculine appeal. Almost against her will, she felt herself moving toward him. Tracy wasn't sure if she should slap him silly or hurl herself into his arms and *kiss* him silly.

Duke made the decision for her. Without saying a word, he stretched his right arm out, inviting her into his embrace.

Nothing could have kept her away. She bolted across the corridor and wrapped both her arms around his waist. A small cry worked its way up her throat as she buried her head in his shoulder.

Duke's good arm came around her, and Tracy felt a sense of peace, a happiness she'd never experienced before.

His cheek moved against her hair, as if he savored the feel of her in his arms. "You're right," he whispered, and his voice didn't sound anything like normal. "I should've told you."

"I nearly had a heart attack when I turned around and saw you in the room."

"I know. I saw that right away. Obviously I wasn't thinking when I went in."

"Then you were gone."

"I meant to leave as soon as I realized what was happening to you, but then you seemed to recover. So I waited till it was nearly over and came out here to wait."

She nodded, breathing in the scent of him. He wore a bay-rum after-shave that made her think whimsically of pirates with rakish smiles and sparkling Caribbean seas.

"You're good, sweetheart, damn good. I always knew you could argue better than any woman I'd ever known, but when you're standing in front of a jury box, you're something to behold."

She was tempted to laugh *and* weep. "You certainly know how to sweet-talk a woman when you have to, Duke."

"That's no bull, Trace. You're a damn good attorney."

"Thank you." But she hadn't even gotten up to half speed! If he could see her when she really hit her stride...

"Will you go to dinner with me?" he asked.

"When?"

He hesitated. "Tonight?"

"Yes," she answered, unable to hide her eagerness. "If you want, you can pick me up at my office. I generally don't get out of there until after six."

"Fine. I'll see you then." He kissed her forehead. His lips lingered against her cool skin. When he released her it seemed hard for him to let her go.

Evening wouldn't come soon enough to suit Tracy.

"I'll be there by six," Duke promised.

Tracy knew that their embrace had attracted a good deal of attention. Many of the people who knew her stared with undisguised curiosity, but Tracy didn't care.

Duke started toward the elevator.

"Duke," she called, and he turned around. "It's good to see you."

He grinned and brushed the hair from his brow. "You too."

She watched him board the elevator while her mind spun with gleeful excitement. Duke in Seattle. And she'd be seeing him again that very evening.

"Who's the hunk?" Janice Cooper, her friend and colleague, had strolled to her side.

"A friend."

"He must be some friend if you practically run into his arms. Weren't you the one who insisted all men are animals but some of them make nice pets?"

"This one's special," was all Tracy would admit. To say anything more would be to give herself away. Although she supposed she'd already done that.

"He must be," Janice added with a hefty sigh of envy. "I don't think I've ever seen you look this happy."

So it showed. Well, Tracy mused, she obviously wasn't very good at hiding her feelings. Somehow she didn't care.

"He looks the rough-and-ready type," Janice continued, "nothing like the type you usually go for. Like Gavin. What makes this one so special?"

"You mean other than the fact that he saved my life?"

Janice released a long low whistle. "*That* was Duke Porter?"

"The one and only."

"But I thought he lived in Alaska."

"He does."

"I suggest you find whatever it is that man's got so we can bottle it. Most of the men I've met in the past ten years could use a solid dose of this guy."

Tracy chuckled, but Janice was right. The men she'd dated fell sadly short on the masculinity index. Duke's muscles weren't built in any gym and what was left of his tan came from the sun. He had the instincts and the natural confidence to cope with any situation. He had courage. He knew who he was, without needing psychiatrists, self-help manuals or courses on finding his inner child.

Duke Porter was as genuine as they came.

DUKE STUDIED his reflection in the store mirror and barely recognized himself. He couldn't recall the last time he'd worn a suit. His father's funeral, he supposed, more than fifteen years ago. It was the same suit he'd worn to his graduation. And his mother's second wedding.

"What do you think?" The salesman circled him like a buzzard, closing in for the kill. The man knew a sale when he smelled one.

Duke checked the price tag dangling from the end of the jacket sleeve. And groaned. Five hundred bucks for a suit seemed a hell of a lot just to be properly dressed to take Tracy out to dinner. When he'd called to make reservations at the hotel's fancy dining room, he'd been informed a tie was required "for the gentlemen." A tie? For dinner? He wondered what they served that was so almighty special that a man was expected to dress up for the experience.

"You can have the alterations finished in an hour?" Duke asked. The sale was contingent on that.

"Yes, of course, for a small fee."

Duke would bet the fee was anything but small, but he had no choice. A man didn't take a city girl like Tracy to dinner just anywhere. For reasons he didn't want to question, he found it important to prove he was as classy as any of the men she routinely dated. True, he preferred to eat at a comfortable place like the Hard Luck Café, but he could hold his own in her sophisticated big-city world.

By the time five-thirty rolled around, Duke Porter's new look was complete. A woman in a beauty shop had cut and blow-dried his hair—Duke hoped the guys back in Hard Luck didn't hear about that. He'd shaved and splashed on some new cologne—a lot of lawyers bought it, the saleswoman told him. If his clean-cut looks didn't affect Tracy, then maybe the cologne would do the trick. He was wearing his new suit and silk tie, his new shoes and carrying a lightweight raincoat over his good arm. Assessing himself in the hotel mirror, Duke decided he looked good. Like a million bucks—but then he'd invested nearly that much in the cause. Tracy was worth it though. He trusted she would appreciate the effort.

He arrived at her office building. The outside might have been a bit stark and forbidding, but the interior was posh, richly decorated in mauves and grays. The way Duke figured, if they could afford to put leather sofas in the waiting room, the firm would be too pricey for the likes of him.

A smartly dressed receptionist unlocked the door and smiled at him. She wore her coat and looked ready to leave for the night.

"I'm here for Tracy Santiago," he announced.

"Mr. Porter?" she asked.

He nodded.

"She's waiting for you."

Duke followed the receptionist down the narrow hallway to Tracy's office. She glanced back at him several times.

"Mr. Porter's here," the woman announced to Tracy, then left—reluctantly, it seemed to Duke.

Tracy rose from her desk with a welcoming smile. But the minute her eyes landed on him her grin faded and her jaw dropped. "Duke?" she asked, squinting at him, "is that you?"

"Hey, I thought you'd like my fancy duds." He held out his right arm and rotated, giving her an eyeful of what five-hundred-plus bucks could buy in this town.

"I can't believe... You look so different," she murmured. Shaking her head, she brought her hands to her mouth. "I can't believe it."

"You mean you don't like it?" He'd be pretty disappointed if that was the case.

"Like it—yes, of course. It's just that you don't...look like you."

He frowned. "Then who the hell do I look like?" He'd never known Tracy to be flustered—other than this afternoon, when he'd surprised her in court. Now that he thought about it, he wasn't exactly sure how he'd expected her to react. She wasn't the type to gush all over him, although, in a way, he supposed he would've liked that.

She walked around from behind her desk and stood before him. "You're probably the handsomest best-dressed man I've ever seen."

The tension eased from Duke's shoulders. Handsomest, best-dressed—now, those were compliments he could live with.

"You don't look bad yourself, sweetheart."

If he didn't know better, Duke would've sworn Tracy blushed. He peered at her carefully—yup, she was definitely blushing. He hadn't thought the man existed capable of cracking this woman's composure, least of all him.

The blush added a tinge of pink to her cheeks, and before he could consider the wisdom of kissing her, Duke lowered his mouth to hers. Tracy angled her head and moaned softly.

Duke's heart boomed like thunder, and he deepened the kiss. After a moment he drew back, trying to clear his head. This wasn't the time or the place for kissing her. "I made dinner reservations," he said in a hoarse voice.

Tracy moistened her lips and lowered her eyes. "I'll get my purse and be ready in just a minute." She reached for her jacket, but Duke took it from her hands.

"Allow me," he said, awkwardly holding it open for her.

She smiled and slipped her arms into the sleeves. "Thank you."

He nodded and resisted the urge to kiss her again. The evening was going to be a test of his restraint if they continued like this. The fact was, he'd prefer to skip dinner altogether and spend the evening making love to her. He found the picture that came to his mind so enticing he had to stop and inhale several deep breaths.

Tracy's office was close to the hotel, so they walked the short distance, holding hands. When he mentioned the name of the restaurant, she arched her brows. "The Rose Garden is one of the most elegant places in town."

"I figured it must be," he said nonchalantly.

The restaurant was on the top floor of the hotel. They rode the elevator up the outside of the building and watched Seattle grow smaller. Tracy pointed out Elliot Bay and Puget Sound.

"I've only been here once," Tracy said. "The food was great, but—" she hesitated and dropped her voice "—very expensive."

"Don't worry," he whispered, "I can afford it."

He nearly changed his mind when he read the prices listed on the menu. Even Alaska didn't charge a man ten bucks for a cup of coffee. He wasn't sure he liked the atmosphere, either. Men running around in fancy dress was one thing, but having the waiter place his napkin in his lap was another. There were some things a man preferred to do on his own!

"What are you having?" Tracy asked. Her eyes met his above the menu.

Duke was a meat-and-potatoes kind of guy. Always had been and always would be. He read the list of dishes offered and couldn't find a solitary thing he'd seriously consider eating. Alligator. Pheasant. Frog's legs. Snails. Duck. The one item that interested him was salmon, but he could have that in Alaska any time he wanted without paying an exorbitant price. Good grief, there were only so many ways to cook a fish.

"Have you decided?" he asked.

A waiter stiffly approached their table, his nose leveled toward the ceiling. He held a pen and pad in his hand and looked distinctly unfriendly. "The special this evening is *palomillo à la parrilla*.'' He paused. ''And may I ask the wine steward to discuss our wine list with you?''

''I believe we'll need a few more minutes,'' Duke said. ''And no, thanks to the wine—I'll just have a beer.''

''Me, too,'' Tracy said, mentioning the name of a local microbrewery.

The waiter seemed not to hear them.

With precision movements, he pivoted and walked away.

''I wouldn't mind a salad,'' Tracy said.

Duke figured he'd be safe if he ordered the same thing. ''That sounds good,'' he said, and set aside the menu.

Tracy ordered the *salade printanière Monte Carlo.*

''I'd like a salad, as well,'' he said, looking the waiter in the eye although he nearly had to stand on the seat of his chair to do so. ''But all I want is some lettuce and maybe a few other vegetables sliced over it.''

''Celery and radishes?'' the waiter suggested.

''Fine.'' Duke was easy to please.

''Alfalfa sprouts?''

''That's fine, too,'' he said, and smiled over at Tracy.

''Asparagus?''

Duke nodded.

''In other words you'll have the *salade printanière Monte Carlo?*''

''Exactly,'' Duke said as if he'd known that all along. He was beginning to think this waiter wasn't interested in receiving a tip.

''Very well, sir.''

Duke returned his attention to Tracy.

''Might I suggest the *scallion vinaigrette* dressing for your salads?'' the man continued.

''Please,'' Tracy answered.

''I prefer ranch dressing.

The man's nose angled even higher. "I'm afraid we don't carry ranch dressing."

"Blue cheese then."

The waiter sighed, clearly disapproving of Duke's choice. "As you wish."

As soon as he left the table, Tracy smothered a laugh. "I'm sorry," she said. "I was just thinking of that waiter working at the Hard Luck Café." She giggled. "He wouldn't last five minutes."

Duke grinned. "At least Ben serves ranch dressing."

"Speaking of Ben, how is he?"

"Doing great. He recently hired a chef, Mrs. Mc-Murphy—"

"A woman?" Tracy asked, elevating an eyebrow.

"Is there something wrong with that?" Duke asked.

"Of course not! It just surprises me. I didn't think Ben was the type who'd let another person in his kitchen—particularly not a woman."

"We Alaska men are a lot more fair-minded than you give us credit for," Duke said, pretending to be insulted. But his eyes caught hers, and soon they were both smiling.

A few moments later, their drinks came in crystal glasses and their salads arrived under silver-domed lids. Duke had eaten plenty of lettuce in his day, but he'd never seen anything so artfully arranged. The asparagus fanned out like a starburst in the middle of the plate. It looked almost too pretty to eat.

"No wonder the prices are so high," he murmured, staring at the vegetables on the gold-rimmed china plate.

"It tastes even better than it looks," Tracy promised, and she was right.

But it wasn't enough. Duke recognized that even as he paid the bill. Once he'd dropped Tracy off at her home, he'd head to the closest hamburger joint and get himself a real dinner.

"How about a walk along the waterfront?" Tracy suggested on the elevator ride down.

"Sure." Duke didn't want their evening to end so soon, even if he felt half-starved.

"I love the Seattle waterfront," Tracy said as they strolled downhill toward Elliot Bay. Friday-night traffic filled the streets, and Duke stared at it, still amazed by the noise and the number of people. He didn't mention that he'd spent much of the day sightseeing. He'd been particularly impressed by the waterfront area—Pike Place Market, the fish market, and the produce stands. Why, there were fruits and vegetables he'd never even heard of before!

Before he returned to Hard Luck, Duke decided, he'd buy a few of the delicacies he'd discovered for his friends. Seedless watermelons would be a sure hit with the youngsters.

"Tell me about everyone," Tracy said as they walked to the end of the pier. The wind whipped her hair about her face. She leaned against the railing, staring out over the choppy green waters. The evening had begun to fade, and the streetlights had come on, casting a warm glow over the area.

"Karen's really looking pregnant these days," Duke commented. "Abbey, too, come to think of it." Tracy had seen both women when she was in town for Mariah and Christian's wedding. It hardly seemed possible that it was only weeks ago; it felt like a lifetime. He'd changed in those weeks. So had she.

"Ben's getting more ornery every day," Duke said with a chuckle. They'd reached the end of the pier.

"Dotty, Sally and Angie?"

"Doing just fine. They send their love." His voice fell on the word *love*.

He had no intention of kissing her with people milling about, but it was asking too much not to hold her. He'd dreamed of little else for too long not to give in to the temptation. Later, he promised himself. Later, he'd kiss her.

With only one good arm, holding her proved to be slightly difficult. He moved closer and slid his arm about her waist.

Tracy placed her hand against his chest, and Duke suddenly decided he didn't want to wait. Slowly he leaned forward and kissed her. He reasoned that it was evening and there weren't *that* many people. Anyone who didn't like it could look elsewhere.

Duke almost lost himself in that kiss. The way she tasted, the way she felt... Somewhere deep inside, he managed to find the restraint to break away.

Tracy trembled, her eyes wide and uncertain. "When... will you be going back?"

That was the sixty-four-thousand-dollar question. Duke didn't know. The way he felt just then, it wouldn't be anytime soon.

"How long are you staying? A few days?"

He heard the dread in her voice and nearly kissed her again. What they were doing wasn't smart; Duke recognized that at the same time he realized he didn't care. Some might call him a selfish bastard, and he'd be the first to agree, but right now, he needed her. He needed this.

"I don't know," he said.

"Longer than a week?" she prompted.

Because he couldn't answer her question, he kissed the delicate curve of her neck. It felt so good to touch her like this, to savor her softness.

"Duke?"

"More than a few days," he whispered.

"A week? Longer?"

Her scent intoxicated him. "Yes," he whispered.

She exhaled softly, and his heart constricted. All these years he'd assumed he had to be ten-thousand feet above the earth to get this high. He'd never realized a man could experience this exhilaration with a woman.

Tracy was teaching him things he'd never known. Never suspected.

The sound of children giggling pulled them apart. Duke took her hand and together they strolled back up the pier.

"There's so much I want to show you," Tracy said.

They passed a fish-and-chip place, and the smoky scent of grilled salmon was enough to make Duke's stomach growl with hunger. Tracy might be satisfied with a mere salad, but a bunch of fancy lettuce decorated with alfalfa sprouts simply didn't fill him.

"You're hungry," Tracy accused.

He shrugged. "A little."

Her eyes lit up with excitement. "I know a fabulous little Mexican restaurant that's just four or five blocks from here. There's not much ambience, but the food is terrific. You game?"

He chuckled and nodded. "What about you?"

"I'm starving," she admitted, smiling broadly.

"Lead the way, woman."

"One thing first," she said. "You'll be in town tomorrow evening?"

Duke nodded.

"Then I'll treat you to dinner."

Duke stiffened. "I don't know how men and women do it here, but in Alaska a man buys."

Disagreement flashed in her eyes, but Tracy didn't argue with him. "What if I cooked the meal myself?"

He hadn't considered that. "You cook?"

She kissed her fingertips and made a loud smacking sound. "You haven't eaten until you've tasted my cooking."

This woman was full of surprises. "I'll be there. Just tell me where and when."

BEN WAS AMAZED at how well the Friday-night special went over with the married folks in Hard Luck. Mary sold out of the prime rib during the first hour. This Friday she'd decided to cook two complete roasts, using his recipe.

For years Ben had catered to the men on Friday evenings. Some of the pipeline workers always flew in for a little rest and relaxation. The guys got a chance to catch up with each other, talk, share a few laughs. It wasn't uncommon for them to play pinochle or bridge, either.

Ben hadn't given much consideration to what the married couples in town did for entertainment. He knew from Bethany that Mitch usually rented a movie from Pete Livengood's store or had one of the pilots pick up a video in Fairbanks. They spent the early part of Friday night in front of the television with a big bowl of popcorn before Mitch, a public-safety officer, went out on patrol.

"You sure we're going to sell enough of the specials to use up both those roasts?" Ben asked Mary.

She nodded. "We could have doubled our sales last Friday, and I've been advertising all week. Don't you worry. If there're leftovers, I'll make roast-beef sandwiches the lunchtime special on Saturday."

Ben didn't have much of an argument. He'd come to trust Mary's judgment and was willing to give her a free hand in most culinary matters.

At six that evening, Sawyer and Abbey showed up, holding hands.

"We're on a date," Sawyer told Ben, and winked at his wife. "The kids insist they're old enough to stay on their own and we're giving them a chance to prove it."

Abbey slid into the booth, and Sawyer sat next to her. Abbey's tummy was growing nice and round these days, Ben noticed. She looked prettier than he'd ever seen her, and he suspected the pregnancy had something to do with that.

No sooner had Abbey and Sawyer seated themselves when Christian and Mariah walked into the café.

"You meet up with the nicest people at Ben's," Abbey teased.

"Do you mind if we join you?" Christian asked.

The two brothers sat across from each other, their wives at their sides. The sight produced a sense of rightness in Ben.

There'd been a time not so long ago that he'd assumed the two older O'Halloran boys would remain bachelors. For some reason, Ben had always thought Christian would marry, but not his older brothers.

Ben was well aware that the women moving to town were responsible for the vast changes in Hard Luck. It astonished him every time he thought about it. Why, their community was growing by leaps and bounds. They'd become a real family town, a good place to raise kids—and to grow old.

Ben spent the evening helping out where he could. He found himself busy, pleasantly so, but not overworked. With his permission, Mary had hired two part-time employees, a couple of high school girls who were excited about the job. She'd trained them herself.

He wasn't sure what it was, but Mary McMurphy had a way about her he didn't fully understand. She'd approach him about a matter he adamantly opposed, and then—before he knew how she'd managed it—he'd find himself agreeing.

Hiring the two part-time waitresses was a perfect example. When she suggested that they needed serving help, he'd decided he would take on one and only one waitress. The funny part was that Mary had accepted his decision and even agreed with it. But before long she'd brought up a number of excellent points on the advantages of hiring additional help. The next thing Ben knew, he had two part-time employees, just what Mary had suggested in the beginning.

The evening went well, and as she predicted, Mary sold out of both roasts. One of the things he liked best about her was that she didn't gloat.

"I'll finish this," he told her when he found her washing up the last of the pans. "You've been here all day."

"Actually," Mary said, drying her hands on a clean towel, "I . . . waited because I had something important to ask you."

Ben noticed that her eyes didn't quite meet his. Hell, the woman hadn't worked for him a month and she was going to demand a raise. Ben could see it coming.

She'd planned this all along, he'd bet. She'd made herself indispensable just so she could turn around and demand all kinds of unreasonable things. He braced himself for the worst.

"What is it?" he asked gruffly.

Mary's head jerked at his tone, and her eyes filled with shock. "I—I wanted to know if you'd mind if I used your kitchen to bake my cinnamon rolls for the Caldwells," she blurted out. "I'd be willing to pay you whatever you felt was fair for the use of the electricity and all."

It was then that Ben noticed tears shining in her eyes.

"Never mind," she said, reaching for her coat. "I should've realized that would be unfair to you. Forgive me, Ben." And she was out the back door before he could stop her.

CHAPTER EIGHT

TRACY STOOD in the middle of her compact kitchen and closed her eyes, groaning aloud. Here it was, almost seven on Saturday night, and she was nowhere near ready. She didn't know what she could've been thinking to invite Duke to dinner. Especially a dinner she'd made herself.

She didn't cook. She'd never cooked an entire meal in her life—at least, not one people could actually eat.

When she'd so blithely said Duke hadn't lived until he'd tasted one of her dinners, she'd been challenging the fates. Opening her eyes, she regarded her normally spotless kitchen and wanted to weep. The room was a disaster. Every pan she owned was filled with one abandoned effort after another.

Sauces—she'd assumed that if she followed a recipe, she could make a decent sauce, not this foul-smelling stuff burned to the bottom of her brand-new saucepan. But the only reason she'd ever used her stove before today was to light candles when she couldn't find matches. All right, that was a slight exaggeration. She'd boiled water and heated canned soup. All her other meals were delivered or came in a package she warmed in her microwave.

She checked her watch and groaned again. Duke would arrive soon, and she didn't know what she'd do then. The sirloin-tip roast had sounded so easy. The butcher had been kind enough to give her detailed directions—a little salt, a dash of pepper, a rub with a garlic clove, then slap it in the oven. The same with the woman at the Pike Place Market where she'd picked up the fresh asparagus. A little water, she'd said, and a pinch of salt. Why, even a child could cook asparagus.

Tracy had paid a king's ransom for these jewels, but the hollandaise sauce she'd intended to pour over them was an unmitigated disaster. She'd really wanted to dazzle Duke with that sauce.

The mashed potatoes were...disgusting. She'd wanted everything to be perfect for Duke, so she'd peeled, boiled and mashed the real thing. Her mistake had come when she'd poured in too much milk. Then, in desperation, she'd attempted to fix her mistake by adding instant potato flakes. Now the sorry mess looked as if it would be better used as wallpaper paste.

As for gravy, hers resembled a watered-down drink from some sleazy bar. Not a thick rich sauce redolent of an expensive cut of meat.

The one bright spot was dessert. She'd been smart enough to pick up a strawberry torte at the bakery. It sat safe and protected on the bottom shelf of her refrigerator.

Her table set with china and crystal looked elegant, Tracy willingly admitted. She'd bought a book that showed how to fold linen napkins and spent a good hour learning how to turn each one into a bird. They sat, poised for flight, on her china plates.

Tracy barely had time to change out of her jeans and into slacks and a silk blouse when the doorbell chimed. She slipped her feet into shoes and looped gold earrings into her earlobes as she hurried to the front door.

Taking an extra second to survey her condominium, she noticed that a magazine had been left out. She raced across the room and hid it under a pillow.

"Duke, hello." She greeted him as though she'd been lazing around all day. Little did he know that she'd spent her entire Saturday on this dinner, agonizing over each detail.

He stepped inside and handed her a bouquet of flowers and a chilled bottle of chardonnay. "How sweet," she said, bringing the rosebuds to her nose. Their scent was light and delicate. Tracy hoped it was enough to overpower the aroma of the scorched egg mixture she'd attempted to turn into hollandaise sauce.

"Make yourself at home," she said, draping the roses across one arm like a beauty queen and tucking the bottle under the other.

He stepped farther into the room and looked around. "Nice digs."

Tracy was proud of her home. The high-rise condominium offered a fabulous view of the islands that dotted Puget Sound. The rooms were spacious, giving the whole place a wide-open feel. She'd purchased it shortly after her first visit to Alaska and realized only later why it had appealed to her so much. The land in Alaska seemed to stretch on forever, and she'd wanted to capture that same sense of freedom in her own home.

Duke walked over to the chrome-and-glass dining-room table and the black lacquered chairs. The table setting was indeed lovely, if she did say so herself.

"Wait here," she said, backing away from him, "and I'll get a vase for the roses. And pour the wine." She didn't dare let him anywhere near her kitchen. The instant he saw the mess she'd created, he'd know the truth.

She opened the swinging door just enough to squeeze her body through and returned a few minutes later. The roses were the perfect complement to her beautiful table.

"Wine?" she asked.

"Please."

Tracy poured them each a glass, then placed the open bottle in an ice bucket on the buffet. With a slightly manic smile, she led the way into the living room.

She sat down in the chair across from him, balancing her wineglass. Tracy feared her perfume hadn't completely covered the scent of smoke in her hair. If Duke got close enough to catch a whiff of that, he'd realize she'd nearly set her kitchen on fire.

Duke leaned toward her as if he felt the distance between them was too great.

"What's for dinner?" he asked enthusiastically. "I'm starved."

Tracy's heart sank, and she swallowed her rising sense of dread. Doing her best to appear calm and serene, she listed her menu in detail. Duke's eyes grew more appreciative with each item.

"I have to admit, you surprise me."

"I do?" she asked, feeling giddy.

"You must have spent all day in the kitchen."

"Nah," she said and gestured weakly with her hand. She sipped her wine, wondering just how she was going to escape this nightmare she'd created. Sooner or later—probably sooner—he'd learn the truth.

"How'd you spend your day?" she asked.

Duke studied his wine. "I went to a custom-house designer in Tacoma and looked at plans."

"You're building a home? In Hard Luck?"

He nodded. "It's one of the things I've been wanting to do for a long time now, but kept putting off. The accident made me realize how much I was looking forward to building it with my own two hands."

"You must know a great deal about carpentry, since your father worked in the trade."

Duke was very quiet for a moment. "How'd you know that?" He looked at her intently.

Tracy boldly met his stare. "How do you think I'd know? You told me."

"When?"

"While we were waiting for the rescue helicopter."

Slowly Duke eased back against the cushion. "Did I by chance mention anything else?"

"Oh, yes."

"Like what?"

"Well, for one thing, your real name is John Wayne Porter, which is how you came to be called Duke."

He sprang to his feet so fast that Tracy's neck snapped up, following his movement.

"I told you that?"

"Is it a deep dark secret you don't want anyone to know?" That seemed downright silly to her.

"Yes . . . no." He rammed the fingers of his right hand through his hair. "Is there anything else . . . I said?" He turned and glared at Tracy, as if he wasn't sure he could trust her.

She shook her head, not mentioning what he'd said about his parents. Instead, she hung her head and swallowed at the tightness in her throat. Silence fell between them while she composed her thoughts. Plainly Duke didn't want her knowing these things about him.

"We were alone, and I was miserably cold and more afraid than I'd ever been in my life," she whispered. Despite her efforts, her voice trembled. "When night fell, I never realized how black and...and suffocating it can feel. You were obviously hurt, but I didn't know how badly. My greatest fear was that you might die before help arrived. I felt so...so utterly helpless."

Tracy held back the emotion, but with difficulty, taking a few moments to calm herself before she continued. "You seemed to sense my panic. When you were conscious, you calmed me with words. You..." She paused and moistened her lips. "You told me about your dad and growing up in Homer and about the time you were ten and decided to play Superman. You tied a bathroom towel around your neck and flew out the upstairs bedroom window."

"I damn near broke my fool neck," he said with a rueful grin.

"But you didn't. You broke your leg, instead."

Duke laughed softly. "It sounds like I developed foot-in-mouth disease out there."

"You don't remember any of it?" How could he have forgotten? It was during those times he'd held her close, sharing not only his body heat, but a part of himself. In retrospect, Tracy didn't know which had offered more comfort, his warmth or his words.

"I remember very little," he answered starkly.

"You don't need to worry, Duke," she assured him, meeting his gaze. "Your confidences are safe with me."

He relaxed. "Not even the O'Hallorans know my real name is John Wayne."

"It's a perfectly good name."

Duke frowned, apparently disagreeing with her. "I suppose I should be grateful I didn't do or say anything really embarrassing."

"You mean like telling me about the women in your life?"

Duke's eyes narrowed.

"You did mention Maureen," she said, despite knowing she should keep her foolish mouth closed.

Duke went pale. "I told you about Maureen?"

"Your first love...er, lover."

"Isn't it time for dinner?"

"We can wait. I've got everything warming in the oven."

"*Tracy...* "

"All right, all right," she said. "I'll shut up, but rest assured you have nothing to fear. Your secrets are safe with me—mostly safe." She set aside her wineglass, got up and headed for the kitchen.

"Did I happen, uh, to mention anything about you?" he was addressing her back.

"About me?" She turned around, pressing one hand dramatically to her chest. Briefly enjoying herself, she let her eyes grow huge. "As a matter of fact, you did."

He waited expectantly.

Once she felt he'd suffered enough, she answered his question. "You claimed I was the sassiest most opinionated woman you'd ever met."

His shoulders fell slack with relief. "You are, no argument there."

"Then you said I had the best-looking legs of any woman you'd ever known." Having said that, she disappeared into the kitchen, leaving the door to swing in her wake.

Her smile died as she viewed the room. She left the sliced meat and mashed potatoes in a warm oven and took the green salad from the refrigerator. This part of dinner should be edible. She'd bought one of those salad-ready packages that had the vegetables already sliced in with the lettuce. She'd wanted to impress Duke with a homemade dressing, but that was a lost cause. The bottled stuff would have to do. She dumped some on and tossed vigorously, splashing the sides of the crystal bowl. At least it was ranch dressing.

She carried the salad to the table. "Would you like to start with this?" she asked.

"Sounds like a good idea.

Tracy smiled sweetly and prayed he'd fill up on salad, because everything else was a mess. She tried to delay the inevitable, but Duke made it clear that he was eager for the main course.

Her heart beating with trepidation, Tracy delivered the meat, potatoes, limp asparagus and gravy to the table. Duke's smile revealed his anticipation.

"I have to admit," he began, reaching for the meat platter, "that I was skeptical when you said you cooked. As far as I'm concerned, keeping a home is becoming a lost art. Too many women don't value domestic skills anymore." He helped himself to a generous portion of sliced roast.

Silently Tracy forked one thin slice onto her own plate.

Next he piled a mound of mashed potatoes on his plate and liberally poured gravy over both.

Tracy held her breath when he sliced into the meat and sampled his first bite. He winked at her and chewed.

And chewed.

And chewed.

An eternity passed before he swallowed, and when he did, she saw the lump slowly move down his throat.

"I—I hope the roast isn't too tough," she said.

"Not a bit," he assured her, but she noticed that he reached for his water glass and drank until it was empty.

Filling her fork with mashed potatoes and gravy, Tracy tried her first taste of the dinner. The potatoes stuck to the roof of her mouth and the burned taste of gravy, which she'd tried to cover with powdered garlic, was so awful it brought tears to her eyes.

Duke was about to take a bite.

"Stop!" she cried, as if the mashed potatoes were laced with arsenic. She stood up, plate in hand.

He hesitated, fork poised in front of his mouth.

"Don't eat that," she shouted, then raced around to his side of the table. He stared at her as if he feared she'd gone mad. Tracy grabbed his plate and rushed into the kitchen to scrape the contents of both plates into the garbage.

The time had come to tell the truth.

Duke was still seated at her beautifully set table when she returned. Rarely had Tracy felt like such a failure—and rarely had she felt so dishonest.

"What you were saying earlier—about women who ignore the domestic skills," she said weakly. "I'm...I'm afraid I'm one of them."

Tracy fully expected Duke to laugh and taunt her. What she didn't expect was silence.

Duke set his napkin on the table and slowly exhaled.

"Say something," she pleaded, sneaking a peak at him.

"Chinese or pizza?" he asked after another moment.

Tracy didn't hesitate. "Chinese."

He grinned. "You know, I would've eaten every bite, then complimented you on your efforts."

"And died in the process," she added. "I don't require that kind of sacrifice from you."

Duke looked away, and Tracy realized he was struggling not to laugh.

"You knew, didn't you?" she said, guessing the source of his amusement.

"I guessed."

"You might've said something," she accused, fighting down an attack of righteous indignation. "Instead, you let me make a fool of myself and—"

"What could I say?"

She didn't know, but she figured he should've been able to think of something, instead of letting her suffer this way.

"I'm honored you were willing to put yourself through this on my behalf. Not every woman would've gone to all this trouble."

"I wanted to impress you."

"You have," he assured her.

"Sure, with how big a fool I can be."

"No," he countered swiftly. He wrapped his good arm around her waist and pulled her onto his lap. Her heart thumped, and a quivery feeling took hold of her stomach. It was like this every time he touched her.

"You know," she said wistfully, "I've never told anyone this, but I always wanted to be a whiz in the kitchen." She wasn't so naive that she didn't know the path to a man's heart was often through his stomach. She'd always scorned cooking as a reactionary pursuit, something that repressed women. She'd always believed she couldn't afford to indulge in traditional female activities. Like cooking... Her rebellious nature had kept her out of the kitchen. Until now.

No man had ever mattered to her more than Duke. Over the years she'd dated lots of men, but she'd never wanted to impress any of them with her culinary talents. Only Duke.

She'd learn, she decided, and feel good about it. She understood now that preparing a meal for someone you loved wasn't demeaning or repressive at all. It was another way of showing your love. *Not* that she'd be trading in her briefcase for an apron on a full-time basis!

MONDAY MORNING Ben came down the stairs from his apartment to find Mary with her arms elbow-deep in bread dough.

"Mornin'," he greeted in the same gruff tone he generally used.

"Mornin'." Mary didn't turn to look at him.

Ben exhaled sharply. They hadn't spoken since she'd rushed out of the café Friday evening. He was a crusty old bachelor who'd managed, amazingly, to offer the men who sought his help advice on romance. But for himself, he wasn't sure how to even *talk* to a woman.

He poured himself a cup of coffee and eyed Mary, wondering where to start. Normally he planned the day's menu, and the two worked companionably together.

"Looks like snow," he said, although he hadn't so much as glanced at the sky.

"Good chance," she returned.

"One year at the beginning of October we got twenty inches in a single day."

Mary made no comment, but continued to knead the dough with practiced hands.

Ben waited—for what, he didn't know. "Dammit, Mary!" he barked.

She jumped at the sound of his voice, increasing his sense of guilt.

"Say something," he ordered.

She finally turned to face him, her eyes flashing fire. "And just what do you want me to say?"

"You wanted to talk to me about baking your rolls for the Caldwells, right?"

"Yes," she returned huffily, "but you made it plain you weren't interested, so I dropped the matter."

"I thought you were going to ask me to give you a raise. I don't want to sound cheap or anything, but you've barely started working here and—"

"A raise?" she cried as if he'd insulted her.

"What else was I to think?"

Mary planted her hands on her hips and glared at him.

Ben knew he owed her an explanation, but he felt awkward making it. He wasn't accustomed to explaining his actions, and it bothered him that he needed to now. "I haven't had many employees over the years."

"So I gathered," she said, and it seemed to him that her voice was a bit less exasperated. "I wasn't asking for any raise, Ben Hamilton. All I wanted to know was if you'd mind if I baked an extra batch or two of my cinnamon rolls for the Caldwells' guests, come winter."

Ben nodded, indicating she should continue.

"Naturally I wouldn't bake during the hours I'd be working for you."

"Naturally," he echoed.

"It would mean staying in town one weekend a month and using the ovens on Saturday mornings. I'll miss visiting my grandchildren, but that can't be helped."

Ben often used the ovens himself on weekends.

"Of course, I'd bake in the morning so you'd have free use of the ovens later in the day."

Ben could see she'd thought the matter through.

"Since I'd be using your kitchen and your ovens," she went on, "I'd be willing to pay you whatever you felt was fair."

"I see. Are the Caldwells supplying the ingredients?"

"No, I'll pay for those myself."

Ben could see a problem in the making. He didn't know how they were going to keep everything separate. Her flour, his flour. Her butter, his butter.

He mentioned this.

"I hadn't thought about that," she murmured.

"Perhaps we could sell the cinnamon rolls as a Hard Luck Café specialty. You could bake while you're on duty here, and we'd divide the profits." As far as Ben could see, his idea offered advantages to them both.

Their eyes met and Mary smiled shyly. "That sounds good."

"Does that mean you agree?" he asked.

"Yes. Thank you, Ben," she said, and returned to her dough, humming softly.

That was what Ben had missed, he realized. The sound of Mary's humming as she worked.

The woman might be skinny, but she knew her way around a kitchen. Furthermore she seemed to know just how to bend his will to her own. And for the first time in his life, Ben didn't object to bending a little.

He'd stopped thinking of Mary as a nuisance. To his surprise, they worked well together. He no longer minded sharing his kitchen with another cook, and the fact that Mary was a woman hardly bothered him at all these days.

NOT ONCE in the week that followed did Duke mention returning to Hard Luck. Tracy didn't press him for fear he'd think she'd grown tired of his company. Nothing could be further from the truth. If anything, she'd come to rely on spending all her spare time with him.

He brought her the plans he'd had drawn up for his house, and together they'd gone over each detail. It amazed her that anyone would undertake such a project, but Duke seemed to know what he was doing. At any rate, he revealed no qualms. According to what he'd told her, he could have the project completed the following summer. True, he'd need help with certain aspects of the construction, but he'd already lined that up.

Tracy was working on a project of her own. She was teaching herself to cook. With the help of a basic cookbook, she practiced making a number of uncomplicated recipes. She didn't let Duke know what she was doing, hoping to surprise him in the near future.

Janice stopped off at Tracy's office just before five-thirty one day.

"You seeing your friend again this weekend?" she asked.

Tracy, fresh from the courthouse, was eager to escape. To her great relief, the trial had ended that afternoon; to her even greater relief, she'd won. Now she looked forward to seeing Duke, with no distractions or obligations to worry about. Before his visit she'd always been one of the last to leave the building. Not anymore.

"Yes," she said, slipping some papers she needed to read into her briefcase. "We're driving to Leavenworth early Saturday morning and spending the day there." Tracy looked forward to the trip with an almost child-like excitement.

"Are you getting serious about this guy?" Janice pressed.

"Getting serious," Tracy repeated. She *was* serious, very serious. Neither one had discussed it, but Tracy knew Duke felt the same way about her.

He must.

Janice crossed her arms and leaned against the side of Tracy's desk. "Gavin asked about you the other day," she mentioned casually.

Gavin seemed like a stranger. Tracy could hardly believe the two of them had once dated. She was astonished that she'd ever seen him as more than a friend.

Gavin took pride in being sensitive to a woman's needs; he always agreed with Tracy on social, political and sexual issues. He kept current on the latest trends and "correct" ideas. He never *argued* with her, never expressed an outrageous opinion. He was a good person, but compared to Duke, he was boring.

Duke wasn't insensitive, Tracy had discovered. The things he'd said and done in the past had been part of a game with him. He'd looked for ways to irritate her, enjoyed sparring with her, delighted in provoking her. Granted, he was a traditionalist and they'd never agree on everything. That, she figured, should keep life interesting for both of them. She understood now that she'd willingly participated in their volleys, that they were an effective way of dealing with her attraction to him. And vice versa, she strongly suspected.

"Tell Gavin I said hello the next time you see him," Tracy replied without giving the matter much thought.

"He asked me out," Janice announced. She seemed to be waiting for Tracy to object.

"I hope you accepted," she said, snapping her briefcase shut.

"I thought I should talk to you first," her friend said, sounding awkward and unsure. "I mean . . . I know you like Duke, but eventually he's going to leave, and then there'll be Gavin again." She flung a stray lock off her shoulder in a gesture that looked like a challenge.

"There'll be Gavin again," Tracy repeated.

"He's crazy about you."

"No, he isn't," Tracy countered, almost laughing. "You just think he is. Listen, Janice, I haven't got time to talk now—I'm meeting Duke. If you want my permission to date Gavin, you've got it."

Janice didn't say anything for several moments. "You're sure you mean it?"

"Absolutely positive."

"What . . . what if things don't work out between you and Duke?"

"They will," she said with utmost confidence. Duke might not know it yet, but he'd learn soon enough. She reached for her briefcase and smiled. "As for Gavin—go get him, Jan. He's all yours."

Her friend returned the brilliant smile. "Thanks, Trace."

"No problem," she said on her way out the door. She should have recognized that Janice was interested in Gavin much sooner, and was sorry it had taken her so long. She had an excuse though; love had blinded her.

THE FOLLOWING MORNING Duke and Tracy headed out of Seattle on their way to the German settlement of Leavenworth. Duke drove her car. Tracy had packed a picnic lunch full of goodies from the deli, and the day stretched before them like an unplanned adventure.

"You're going to love this," Tracy assured him. "The entire town celebrates Octoberfest."

"The only Leavenworth I've ever heard of is a prison," he mumbled, and took his eye off the road long enough to glance her way.

"This is no prison," Tracy said, then went on to describe the town with its elaborate old-European buildings. "It's like stepping into a fairy tale," she concluded.

Duke frowned. "A fairy tale. We're driving three hours for that?"

"A fairy tale with beer," she amended.

Duke grinned. "Now you're talkin'."

Tracy rested her head against his shoulder. "The most amazing thing happened to me last night," she said, remembering her short conversation with Janice.

"Oh?"

"My friend—a good friend, at that—asked me if I minded if she went out with Gavin."

"Mr. Sensitive?"

"Right."

"What did you tell her?"

Tracy thought she heard an edge in Duke's voice. He was jealous and she loved it. "There's no need to worry."

"I'm not worried," he insisted. But when she didn't continue the conversation, he prodded her. "Aren't you going to tell me your answer?"

"I thought you weren't worried."

"I'm not, but I'll admit to being mildly curious. After all, this is the very man you used to toss in my face as a paragon of virtue."

"Oh, hardly."

"You most certainly did," he said with ill-disguised impatience.

"As far as I'm concerned, Janice is free to do with Gavin whatever she wishes."

Duke gave her a cocky smile. "That's what I though"
you'd say."

"Oh, are we getting overconfident or what?" she
teased.

"No," he answered simply. "I don't have any hold or
you. You can see whoever you please. It just so happens
I please you."

At one time, not so distant, his words would have in
flamed her. Now they amused her.

She was surprised when Duke grew quiet. She enjoyee
the playful banter they often shared.

"Tracy," he said, his voice harsh with regret, "I've go
to get back to Hard Luck."

She opened her mouth to protest and knew it would do
no good. He'd already stayed far longer than she had an
right to hope.

"Trust me, sweetheart, I don't want to go, but I hav
to."

"When?" she asked, fighting down her dread.

"Soon. In a couple of days."

"When will I see you again?"

He shook his head. "I don't know. I don't get dow
this way very often."

"I probably won't be able to fly up to Hard Luck un
til spring." And spring seemed a million years away
Tracy couldn't bear the thought of waiting until the ic
broke on the rivers before she saw Duke again.

The silence between them grew oppressive. "There"
one option," she said.

"You mean meeting halfway? I've thought about tha
and—"

"No." She cut him off, thinking fast. Her ey
rounded with excitement. "There's another way."

"I've thought about it over and over," Duke said, sounding discouraged, "and I can't come up with anything."

"But, Duke, did you ever consider the obvious?" She paused. "We could get married!"

CHAPTER NINE

"MARRIED?" DUKE DAMN NEAR drove off the road. He couldn't believe his ears. Married? Him? To Tracy? The woman needed her head examined.

First, he wasn't the marrying kind. Never had been, never would be. Second, Tracy? And *him?* A polished city woman and an outdoors guy? A sophisticated attorney and a down-and-dirty Alaskan bush pilot? No way!

"Well?" Tracy said excitedly, studying him. "What do you think?"

Duke opened his mouth, but no sound came out. Myriad objections tangled themselves on the end of his tongue. Then, because he couldn't formulate a clear response, he said tartly, "In case you need reminding, there are certain things the man does in a relationship, and proposing marriage is one of them."

"Fine. I'm all ears." She laid her head on his shoulder, and the warm feelings he'd experienced every time they were together, every time they touched, continued. He should have realized when he saw the stars in her eyes what she was thinking in that brilliant mind of hers. Not for the first time he wanted to slap himself upside the head for even making this trip to Seattle. All he'd managed to do was set them up for trouble.

Marriage. That was the way a woman's mind worked. Duke had assumed, had hoped, that a career-oriented woman like Tracy would be different. She wasn't.

"I'm waiting," she said, and smiled up at him, her eyes so bright they nearly blinded him.

Duke swallowed uncomfortably. "Sweetheart, listen, you don't know what you're saying."

"I most certainly do," she insisted.

Duke should have known he was walking onto a tightrope without a safety net, but he knew he couldn't avoid the subject. "It's only natural that you should feel close to me, seeing what we've been through. But it's not enough to..." He let his words trail off. Yes, they shared a closeness that went beyond the usual male-female relationship. They'd faced death and had bonded in ways that took most folks years to achieve. And while it was true he harbored few of the resentments he'd originally felt toward Tracy, he wasn't anywhere close to considering marriage to her.

"In other words, you don't feel anything special for me, even though—"

"I didn't say that," he interrupted.

"Then explain yourself, Duke Porter." She raised her head from his shoulder, and sat up straight as a pool cue, sliding closer to the passenger door.

"Let's discuss this later," he suggested, wanting to delay the argument until they'd both had time to give the subject some rational thought. But he knew that no matter how much thinking he did, he wasn't going to change his mind. Any kind of long-term arrangement between them was impossible. For many reasons.

"I'd prefer that we talk about it now," Tracy persisted.

He should've known she wasn't going to let it drop this easily. Figuring it would be impossible to talk about this *and* drive safely, he exited the freeway. He didn't know the name of this city, only that it was north of Seattle. He followed the signs to the city park.

Neither spoke until he pulled into the parking lot and turned off the engine. There were trees everywhere, their leaves brilliant shades of orange and red, but Duke barely noticed.

"All right," he said, and expelled his breath slowly, dreading what was sure to come. "Since you insist, let's air this here and now."

"You make it sound like we're about to put up our dukes and fight." She paused and smiled thinly. "No pun intended."

Grateful for her light remark, Duke grinned. Maybe they could both laugh off the marriage suggestion. It would save her pride and his freedom.

Sure he loved her; he was willing to admit that. He loved her as much as he did any woman, possibly more. All right, *probably* more, but that still didn't mean he was ready to settle down for the rest of his life.

"Marriage? Really, Tracy, can't you see that it'd be a disaster with us?"

"No," she answered fiercely.

"Sweetheart, think about it. You and me? We're different people."

"I should hope so."

This wasn't going well. Not well at all. Already he could feel the noose tightening around his neck, and he wasn't going to let that happen. He tried a different approach.

"We live in different worlds. I don't fit in yours, and you sure as hell don't fit in mine."

"I love Hard Luck," she said, her tone heartfelt.

"Sure, it's a great town—I couldn't agree with you more. But your work is here and mine is there. I've enjoyed my time in Seattle, but if you didn't live here, I'd've left within a couple of days." He took a deep breath. "I don't deal well with this many people around me twenty-four hours a day. I need elbow room, and lots of it."

"I'm not asking you to move to Seattle," she said.

"You're not suggesting you move to Hard Luck, are you?" Try as he might, Duke couldn't picture Tracy living in the Arctic.

"That's exactly what I'm saying."

"Tracy," he said, laughing softly, "have you lost your mind?"

Her eyes held his for a long time. "No," she whispered. "I've lost my heart. I love you, Duke. I want to spend the rest of my life with you. I want to help you build that house you've planned, and then, God willing, I want us to fill those bedrooms with children. Our children."

Her words fell like a sword, cutting him to the bone. His mind immediately filled with the sound of children's laughter, and the allure was so strong he was forced to close his eyes and concentrate in order to banish it.

Home. Children. Damn, she was good, but then Duke knew that; after all, he'd seen her in action in a courtroom.

But it wouldn't work, not this time. If she didn't recognize that, then he did.

Duke had tried to be part of her world, and it had cost him five hundred dollars for a suit he'd probably never wear again. He'd been snubbed by an arrogant waiter because he preferred ranch dressing. He'd never paid more for a few leaves of lettuce, even in Alaska, than he had in that fancy restaurant. He'd done all that in an effort to impress Tracy, and the only thing he'd gained—he suspected it was a bargain—was the realization he'd never be comfortable in the big city.

For her part, Tracy had tried to fit into his life, too. If he'd ever doubted she loved him, all he had to do was remember the dinner she'd slaved over on his behalf.

If he didn't love her as much as he did, he would've laughed himself silly that night. As it was, he'd been determined to chew every bite, smile and compliment her even if it killed him. And if the first taste was a sample of what was to follow, it just might have.

Tracy living in Hard Luck? As much as Duke enjoyed the notion, he was smart enough to realize it wouldn't work. Besides, there were other more obvious considerations.

"Your career is here in Seattle," he reminded her.

"I can get licensed to practice law in Alaska."

He didn't want to argue with her. It seemed pointless to tell her there wasn't enough work to keep even one attorney employed in Hard Luck. And any cases there were would be minor stuff—wills, maybe a few contracts—not the exciting criminal cases she'd trained for.

She might assume she loved him now, especially in light of what they'd been through together, but that attraction would soon wear off. Once she was subjected to everyday life during an Arctic winter, she'd grow bored and restless. The last thing he wanted was for Tracy to marry him and then regret it later.

As gently as he could, Duke said, "It won't work. I wish to hell I was different, but I'm not. I can't move to Seattle, and you'd never be happy in Hard Luck."

She opened her mouth to argue, but he stopped her. "Hear me out. If ever I was tempted to marry anyone, it would be you. But you're missing the entire point.

"I believe in family, but I like my life just the way it is. I'm free to go where I want, when I want, without the responsibility of a wife or kids. And frankly that's the way it's going to stay."

"I don't intend to lock you away in a closet for the rest of your life," she snapped.

Duke could see that he was waging a battle of words against an expert. Tracy was capable of swaying a twelve-person jury with her arguments. He didn't stand a chance if he continued.

"Listen," he said, his voice gaining strength and conviction, "you took it upon yourself to ask, although I consider that the man's prerogative. Okay, then I suggest you be 'man' enough to accept my answer, and that answer is no. I don't *want* to be married, and I'm not going to let you persuade me otherwise. Understand?"

"Perfectly," she answered in a clipped voice.

Duke immediately regretted the harsh words. "I didn't mean to hurt you." He wanted to kick himself for flying to Seattle and giving in to the need to see Tracy. If anyone was to blame for this fiasco, he knew where to look.

The mirror.

LANNI O'HALLORAN was as nervous as she was excited. Charles was due home that afternoon after three weeks in the field.

She'd known long before they were married that, as a geologist, he was required to make these trips. The first few months of their marriage he'd managed to make it home every few days. Not this time. Charles had been gone a full twenty-one days, and it'd felt like that many years to Lanni.

In an effort to exhaust her emotional energy, she cleaned house and planned a gourmet dinner. But it wasn't food Charles would be thinking about when he walked in that door, and Lanni knew it.

A soft smile touched her lips.

So much had happened in the time he'd been away. She'd sold another article, this time to a glossy women's magazine. With extra time on her hands, she'd dabbled in writing fiction. She wasn't sure how successful it was. But her sister-in-law, Karen, had read the short story and liked it.

There was far more important news than her most recent sale, though. News she couldn't wait to share with her husband.

Lanni glanced at the clock and sighed, wishing the hands would move faster.

Every time a car drove past the house she found herself racing to the front window, hoping it was Charles.

Her news wouldn't keep much longer. She felt it would burst forth the minute he walked in. It wasn't every day a wife could announce she was pregnant.

She'd kept the information to herself a full seven days now, and she was finding secrecy more and more difficult. But it didn't seem fair to share her excitement with her friends when her own husband didn't know.

Lanni knew Charles had wanted to wait until they were married a full year before she became pregnant, and she'd agreed. But eight months was *close* to a year.

Their original plan had sounded good—until Karen had come to Hard Luck, pregnant, and Lanni found herself longing to have a baby herself.

Her brother, Matt, and Karen had been divorced at the time Karen discovered she was carrying Matt's baby. She'd served as Lanni's maid of honor at the wedding, and things had progressed from there. Really, everything had worked out beautifully. There was no telling how long it would've taken those two to come to their senses if not for the pregnancy.

Within a couple of months, Matt and Karen were back together again and they'd remarried soon afterward.

No sooner had Lanni heard the happy news about Karen's baby when Charles's brother, Sawyer, informed them Abbey was pregnant.

Sawyer and Abbey were ecstatic. Sawyer continued to walk two inches above the ground and had from the minute Abbey told him the news. The last Lanni had heard, Sawyer had purchased a case of cigars and was handing them out to his friends. Even though their daughter wasn't born yet!

Charles had been pleased for his brother and Abbey, but he'd still felt they should wait the full year.

Waiting wasn't Lanni's strong suit. She'd agreed to postpone the wedding for eight painful months while she finished her apprenticeship with the Anchorage daily newspaper. Charles didn't want her to regret their marriage and had insisted she complete the program. She'd done it, but had been miserable a lot of that time, missing him dreadfully.

The door swung open. Lanni couldn't believe she hadn't heard the truck. Charles stood just inside their living room, as compellingly virile and handsome as ever. No, more so.

"Charles!"

He dropped his backpack onto the carpet and held out his arms. Lanni didn't need any further encouragement. She raced across the room and hurled herself into them. Even after eight months of marriage, her heart felt as if it would explode with joy at the love she saw in his eyes.

Charles gathered her in close. Even before she could speak, his mouth found hers in a kiss potent enough to buckle her knees. He said with that one kiss how lonely he'd been, how much he'd missed her, how glad he was to be home.

He groaned deeply and urged her mouth open wider. The kiss went on and on, and probably would have lasted even longer if Lanni hadn't been bursting with news.

She pulled her lips from his. "Charles, I've got wonderful news."

"Later," he said, lifting her from the floor and bringing her mouth level with his. "What have you done to me, woman?" he whispered, repeatedly kissing her lips. "I've never missed anyone so much in my life."

"Good. Now you know how I've felt."

"I need a shower," he said, securely wrapping his arms around her waist.

"Dinner's in the oven."

"It's not food that interests me," he said, and chuckled.

"I've been your wife long enough to know exactly where your interests lie, Charles O'Halloran." She braced her hands against his shoulders. "Now, look at me, because I've got something important to tell you."

"You made another sale?" he guessed.

"Yes, but that's not it." Tears of joy filled her eyes and she cupped his face with her hands. "I . . . we're going to have a baby."

Apparently her news shocked him, because his hold slackened and he released her. She slid down his front and landed with a thud on her own two feet. Dismay widened his eyes.

"I know you wanted to wait a full year," she rushed to say, "but we've been married over eight months."

Charles walked to the ottoman and literally slumped into it. "Pregnant?" Almost immediately he was back on his feet. "I need a drink." He walked into the kitchen and brought down a whiskey bottle from the cupboard above the stove.

Lanni followed him, nervously rubbing her palms together. "I . . . I thought you'd be happy."

He looked at her as if he hadn't heard a word she'd said, then poured a liberal amount of the amber liquid into a glass. He tossed it back, then gritted his teeth. "A baby?"

Lanni nodded. "Don't look so shocked. We've been playing Russian roulette with birth control for weeks. Exactly what did you expect would happen?"

"Who else knows about this?"

"No one yet. I wanted to tell you the news first. I thought you'd be happy," she said again.

He shook his head. "I am. It's just that . . ."

"Just what?" she challenged.

"A shock."

"Well, maybe you should receive another," she blurted out. Whirling around, she grabbed her coat and rushed out of the house.

"Lanni!"

She heard him call her name, but ignored it and raced down the street. She'd only gone a short distance when Mariah, driving Christian's truck, pulled up alongside her. She rolled down the window on the driver's side.

"Lanni," she asked, "is everything all right? I thought Charles would be home by now."

"He is."

"What are you doing out in this cold with just a jacket?"

Lanni looked at her sister-in-law and burst into tears. Unable to speak, she wrapped her arms around herself and sobbed.

"You'd better come with me," Mariah said quietly. Leaning over, she opened the passenger door.

Lanni climbed into the truck just in time to avoid Charles, who'd come running after her. She heard his frantic cry, but ignored him.

"Lanni?" Mariah asked gently when she pulled up in front of the house she shared with Christian.

"How about a cup of tea?" Lanni asked, wiping the tears from her face.

"Tea?" Mariah glanced over her shoulder. "Sure. Come inside and you can tell me what's made you so unhappy."

"Unhappy? Me?" Lanni cried. "I couldn't be happier! Charles and I are going to have a baby." As soon as she finished, she started to weep all over again.

CHARLES FIGURED he'd give Lanni a half hour before he went after her. He'd seen her climb into Mariah's car. Right this moment, she was probably telling Mariah and Christian what a bastard he was, and she'd be right.

A baby. Lanni pregnant. It still didn't seem real.

What Lanni had said about playing Russian roulette with birth control was true, but she'd never made a secret of the fact that she wanted a baby. Maybe he was being selfish, but Charles had wanted to keep Lanni to himself for a while longer.

He rubbed a hand across his eyes and considered what he'd done. Lanni was hurt and confused. Hell, so was he.

Charles had never expected to fall in love. When he did, he fell for the granddaughter of the woman who'd spent a large part of her life working to destroy his family. He hadn't known that at first, though. When he *had* learned the truth about her, Charles had turned his back and walked away.

He'd soon learned that was a mistake. He loved her, and with his mother's help and Lanni's persistence, he was able to put aside his doubts. Lanni's love was the greatest gift of his life.

Once again, Charles thought in near-despair, he'd found a way to destroy what he wanted most. After an hour it was clear that Lanni wasn't coming back. He'd need to swallow his pride and go after her. But before he made another colossal mistake, he decided to do what he always did when he needed advice. He visited Ben Hamilton at the Hard Luck Café.

Ben was busy in the kitchen when Charles arrived.

"Long time, no see," Ben greeted him when Charles slid onto a stool at the counter. It surprised him how busy the place was. In the past there'd been times Charles would stop in and be the only customer.

Today Ben actually had a waitress there, and furthermore, he needed her.

"What can I get you?"

"How about a psychiatrist?"

Ben laughed and automatically filled Charles's mug with coffee. "What happened?"

"Lanni's pregnant."

Ben eyed him speculatively. "That's great news, isn't it?"

Charles nodded without a lot of enthusiasm.

"You don't look too sure," Ben said, leaning against the counter.

"I don't know that I'm ready for a family. Dammit, Ben, I love my wife and I wanted her to myself for a few more months." He wasn't going to be the type of father Sawyer was, Charles realized. His brother had wanted to get Abbey pregnant from the moment he'd slipped a ring on her finger.

"Are you saying the baby's due this week?" Ben asked. "I know you're a real go-getter, but this kind of thing usually takes a few months, doesn't it?"

"Yes, but— Oh hell, I suppose you're right. Anyway, I didn't throw my arms into the air and leap for joy the way Lanni expected, and now she's spitting nails she's so mad at me."

"What are you going to do about it?" Ben asked.

Charles stared into his coffee. "The only thing I *can* do. Throw myself at her feet and beg for forgiveness."

"Lately I've noticed," Ben said thoughtfully, "that the longer you wait to apologize, the more difficult it becomes. After a while, the words tend to stick in your throat. Trust me, the sooner you apologize, the better it'll go for you both."

Charles agreed. He glanced at his watch and headed over to Christian's house. He parked out front and sat with his hands resting on the steering wheel while he rehearsed what he intended to say.

Ben was right. The sooner he apologized the better. With a certain reluctance, he climbed out of the truck and knocked on the front door.

Christian answered, looking at Charles as if he should be arrested. "I wondered how long it'd take you to get here." His brother unlatched the screen door and held it open.

Charles stepped inside. "Where's Lanni?"

"In the kitchen with Mariah. What the hell did you say to her?" Christian demanded.

Charles glared at him. "That's between Lanni and me."

"Fine," Christian muttered, "then you go take care of it. She hasn't stopped crying since she got here."

Charles took a deep calming breath and made his way into the kitchen. Lanni sat at the table with her back to him; Mariah sat across from her. He saw a teapot and two cups on the blue checked tablecloth.

"I'd like a word with my wife," Charles said to his sister-in-law. "Alone." It seemed Mariah was going to ignore him, but apparently she changed her mind, because she slipped silently out of the kitchen.

"Lanni," Charles whispered. She didn't respond. He walked over to where Mariah had been sitting and stood behind the chair. He slid his hands into his pants pockets.

Lanni's tear-streaked face made him realize he loved her beyond life itself. He'd wanted everything to be perfect for her, for them. Yet he was the one responsible for her unhappiness. His gut clenched with remorse.

"We're going to have a baby," he said. Now that the information was beginning to sink in, he found he rather liked the idea. A baby. His and Lanni's.

"I know you're not happy about this and—"

"I *am* happy," he insisted, cutting her off. "It just took some getting used to. We're going to have a baby," he repeated. Yes. This was *good* news.

Lanni gnawed on her lower lip. "You aren't angry?"

"Angry?" She'd thought he was angry? He moved around the table and knelt down in front of her. "Never that, honey. Surprised, shocked, but never angry. This is our baby, yours and mine. I'm sorry I reacted the way I did. Can you forgive me?" The words came straight from his heart.

Lanni's eyes brightened with tears and she nodded. "Yes. I'm so happy I could burst."

"I'm happy, too, because you are. The idea of being a father frightens me a little, I admit." But then, it had taken him a long time to get comfortable with the idea of loving Lanni. He knew he was going to love this child beyond reason, the same way he did his wife.

"I love you, Charles," Lanni whispered, throwing her arms around his neck. She rested her head against his shoulder. He didn't deserve her love, but then he'd always known that.

Charles breathed in her fresh scent and buried his face in her neck. Everything was going to work out just fine. Next spring he was going to be a father.

He smiled.

DUKE PUSHED the food around his plate with his fork, his appetite almost nonexistent. He'd been back in Hard Luck for better than two weeks now, but it seemed more like two years.

If he couldn't fly soon, he wouldn't be worth a damn.

"More coffee?" The young waitress Ben had hired had approached his table.

"No, thanks." Duke pushed his plate aside.

"What's the matter, don't you like my spaghetti anymore?" Ben asked. He pulled out a chair and sat down. Before, Duke had always welcomed Ben's company, but these days he preferred his own.

"Guess I don't have much of an appetite," Duke muttered.

"I understand you've bought some land off the O'Hallorans?"

Duke nodded. "I hope to start building soon."

Ben's eyes showed his approval. "A man should have a place of his own."

"It's time I moved out of the bunkhouse," Duke said without further comment. He'd meant to leave a long time ago, but there'd been no compelling reason. Besides, he got along well with the other pilots. Or used to. Right now he didn't think anyone would regret his leaving, not after the last six weeks. He hadn't been good company.

"Seems like a mighty big house for just you. How many bedrooms you planning?"

"Four," Duke answered. Bedrooms. He remembered Tracy's comment about filling those rooms with children and the two of them building a life together. When she'd first mentioned marriage, his hackles had gone up and he'd thought she was crazy. Married? Him? No way.

"Four bedrooms," Ben echoed. "What're you planning to do—open a boardinghouse?"

"No," Duke replied, annoyed. He wasn't sure *what* madness had possessed him to want to build a four-bedroom house when all he required was one bedroom, possibly two.

Ben chuckled. "You got the look, pal."

"The look?" Duke asked.

"Misery. I know all about that broken arm of yours, but it's not physical pain I'm talking about."

"Ben, I appreciate—"

"No, you don't," Ben interrupted. "You resent me like hell right now, and frankly I don't blame you. I've been watching you ever since you got back from Seattle."

"I don't want to talk about Seattle," Duke said tightly. That was the last thing he wanted to talk about—his time with Tracy. She haunted him, every minute of every hour, asleep or awake. It was even worse now than before he'd gone to see her.

"No," Ben agreed, "I don't suppose you do want me to mention your visit to Seattle."

"Furthermore, I'm not the marrying kind."

"That's what Sawyer said, remember? Charles, too, if you recall."

"Well, sure," Duke said, "but they didn't fall in love with a successful big-city attorney, either. It isn't going to work between Tracy and me, and the sooner everyone accepts that, the better."

He knew he sounded angry, but dammit, he was. It might seem straightforward enough from the outside looking in, but Duke had seen Tracy in her element, and it was a lot better than anything he could offer her in Hard Luck.

"You sure about that?" Ben pressed.

"Of course I am," Duke said. He shoved back his chair and stood. "Listen, Ben, I appreciate what you're trying to do, but this time it won't work. Besides, if you're such an expert on romance, you should keep track of what's happening in your own backyard."

Ben frowned. "What do you mean?"

Duke picked up his tab. "Anyone with eyes can see what's going on with you and Mary McMurphy."

Ben's jaw sagged open so far it nearly landed on the tabletop. "You're out of your mind."

Duke chuckled. "If you say so."

"Me and Mary McMurphy?" Ben managed a laugh, but it sounded false. "I'm not in love with her."

"If you say so," Duke repeated, walking toward the cashier and paying his bill.

"I don't want you spreading rumors, you hear me?" Ben warned. "The last thing I want is someone embarrassing Mary with that kind of talk."

"My lips are sealed, Ben. But I have to tell you, I don't think this is much of a secret. The entire town's talking about you two, and everyone's happy for you."

"Mary McMurphy?" the cook scoffed loudly, causing several patrons to turn and stare at him. "There's nothing between me and her!"

At that moment Mary stepped out from the kitchen. Her gaze met Ben's, and even Duke could read the fury and betrayal in her eyes. Then she whirled around and returned to the kitchen. Ben swallowed uncomfortably and glanced longingly in her direction. "A woman like Mary McMurphy is better off without the likes of me," he muttered.

All love did, Duke decided as he walked out the door, was make people miserable. He wanted nothing more to do with it.

CHAPTER TEN

MARY TOLD HERSELF she was nothing but an old fool. Certainly she'd never intended to fall in love with Ben Hamilton. That old sea dog wouldn't know love if it hit him right between the eyes.

Which it had.

Ben had all but shouted his lack of feelings for her to the entire restaurant, humiliating her. Well, at least she knew now exactly where she stood with the man.

Everything they'd shared these past weeks meant nothing. It had seemed to her that they'd come far, but apparently not. She slammed closed the oven door, angry with herself for losing control of her heart when she was old enough to know better.

In the beginning Ben had deeply resented her. He'd made it quite clear that he didn't want her anywhere near his precious kitchen. Gradually his attitude had changed for the better, but it had taken weeks to gain his trust and admiration.

At first, aware of how he felt about her, Mary had tiptoed around his ego, being ever so careful not to take matters into her own capable hands. She knew a thing or two, seeing that she'd been in the restaurant business for well over twenty years. But each and every step of the way, she'd gone to him, seeking his counsel and approval before making changes.

After a time Ben had come to appreciate her suggestions. Her idea of serving prime rib on Friday nights had been a huge success. He'd allowed her to try out a few of her other ideas, as well. Even though he didn't feel the café had enough business to justify hiring two part-time waitresses, he'd agreed to give it a try. Business had increased dramatically, and he'd soon recognized the wisdom of adding additional staff.

It wasn't that Ben didn't appreciate her. Mary knew otherwise. His voice was often gruff, but he had a kind generous heart. It was when she realized this that she'd gradually lowered her guard. That, unfortunately, had proved to be a mistake, because she'd gone and done something foolish. She'd fallen in love with Ben Hamilton.

She'd been a widow for nearly fifteen years now and had given up the idea of remarrying. She was content with her life, but she would've welcomed a companion. A partner.

Her children were grown and didn't need her, so she'd hoped to relax a bit and travel some. Fanciful dreams, she mused sadly. That was all they were. Dreams.

"Mary."

She continued washing the last of the pots and pans. Forcing a smile to her lips, she turned to greet Ben as if nothing was amiss.

"Maybe you and I should sit down and talk," he suggested hoarsely.

You didn't spend this much time with a person and not know him, and Mary sensed Ben's reluctance.

"I don't have time to chat this evening," she returned stiffly. "Perhaps another time."

His shoulders sagged with relief. "Good. I mean, that's okay. Whenever you've got a free moment."

Mary returned to the task at hand, scrubbing the pots with enough force to rub holes clean through them. Her elbow made jerky movements as she expended her anger. And angry she was. Not at Ben. She knew he was uncomfortable with emotion, particularly if it related directly to him. No, she was angry at herself.

Ben cleared his throat and addressed her back. "I did think," he said, "that it was time we discussed giving you a raise."

"I've only been with you a couple of months," she said dismissively, not bothering to turn around again.

"I know that," he snapped, then gentled his voice. "But you've made some good suggestions. Business is better than it's ever been. Your prime-rib special on Friday nights fared a lot better than my frequent-eater program."

She rolled her eyes. Frequent eaters! My heavens, what had the man been thinking?

"I believe a ten-percent increase would be fitting."

Mary was well aware that the raise had been prompted by nothing more than good old-fashioned guilt. He was sorry for embarrassing her.

"I appreciate the offer," she told him firmly, her back still to him, "but no, thanks."

"You're turning down a raise?" Ben sounded incredulous.

"Yes." Mary was sure he'd never heard of such a thing, and in fact, she'd never rejected a raise before. But she did now with good reason.

"Why in tarnation would anyone refuse a raise?" Ben demanded.

Mary pulled the plug in the sink, and the water gurgled down the pipe. Peeling the rubber gloves from her hands, she turned to face him, but kept her gaze lowered.

"Is there anything wrong with my money?" he asked in the same impatient tone he'd used earlier.

"No, except when you're using it as an attempt to buy an apology."

"What do I have to apologize for?" he asked, his voice rising. "You try to do something nice for someone, and what do you get?"

"Now listen here, Ben Hamilton, it's a free country, and I can choose what I will and won't accept as a wage," she said, squaring her shoulders and boldly meeting his look. His face was flushed, and she was sure that losing his temper couldn't be good for his heart condition.

Ben ripped the apron from his waist and flung it aside. "What do you want from me?"

His question took her by surprise. "What makes you think I want anything?"

"Because that's the way women are."

"Really, Ben," she said dryly. "And since when did you become such an expert on women?"

He took a deep breath, which he slowly released, his cheeks billowing out. "I suppose you're going to hand in your notice now."

She'd considered it, but had quickly changed her mind. She'd come to enjoy life in Hard Luck, to love the town and its people. Weeknights were spent at the Caldwells' lodge, and she'd formed friendships with several of the older women in town. "I see no reason to quit—unless you don't want me around any longer."

"I do," Ben admitted gruffly. "Want you around, that is."

The tension left Mary's shoulders and she smiled softly. "Thank you for that."

Ben shifted his weight from foot to foot. "I'd miss you if you decided to move on," he admitted, his gaze holding hers. "I never thought I'd say that, but it's the truth."

"I'd . . . miss working with you, too."

The expression in his eyes grew warm. "I've never been married."

"I know." She'd asked Bethany about his marital status the first week she'd come to work with him.

"I, uh, never gave the matter of marriage much thought," he continued, his gaze skirting past hers. "Women these days want to be romanced. Hell, I'm too old and too fat for that sort of thing. And if the truth be known, I don't know a damn thing about love."

"You most certainly are not old and fat," Mary said heatedly. "You're a fine-looking man. And you say you don't know about love, but that's simply untrue. You're a generous giving human being. Why, this entire community loves you!" She paused, then went on softly, "Your café's the heart of the town. When folks have a problem, you're the one person they seek out for advice."

"Maybe," he agreed reluctantly, "but no woman would ever love a man like me."

"Fiddlesticks." Mary felt like stamping her foot. "That's the most ridiculous thing I've ever heard you say."

Ben studied her, his gaze intense. "What about someone like you, Mary? Could you . . . love me? Would you be willing to marry me?"

"Of course I would! But marriage is more than romance—it's a partnership. It's working together, sharing each other's joys and sorrows. It's building dreams and—" She stopped abruptly when she realized what he'd asked. "What did you say just now?" Her head and her heart felt light with wonder.

Ben drew in a deep breath. "I asked if you'd marry a man like me."

"Is that a proposal, Ben Hamilton?"

He frowned and said nothing.

"You asked if I'd marry a man like you, right?" she prompted irritably.

He still looked stunned. "Did I?"

"Don't worry, Ben, I didn't take you seriously."

"But what you said, about marriage being a partnership, that's true, isn't it?"

"Of course."

"And you said you *would* marry me." He grinned now, obviously taking to the idea.

"I did?"

"I heard you with my own two ears." His smile faded, and he cleared his throat. "Would you be my wife, Mary McMurphy? My partner not only here at the café but in my life?"

Mary felt tears crowd her eyes. She didn't need to think about her response; she already knew. She nodded. "Yes. Oh, yes, Ben."

His face broke into a big smile, and he held his arms open wide for her. Mary felt young all over again as she walked into his embrace. Ben wrapped his beefy arms around her and sighed deeply. To Mary, it was the most romantic sound she'd ever heard.

TRACY GAVE DUKE two weeks. She figured that within that time, he'd come to his senses and realize they were meant to be together. She marked Halloween on her calendar and waited impatiently to hear from him. Only she hadn't.

The man's pride was a formidable thing, she thought as she unlocked her front door and stepped inside. Now it was Halloween night, and the only visitors she could expect were trick-or-treaters. In the morning she'd decide what to do next.

She glanced through her mail and tossed the junk and the bills on her desktop. Mariah had written her a long newsy letter earlier in the week, which Tracy had read through a dozen times or more. Duke's cast was off his arm, and the entire town of Hard Luck had breathed a collective sigh of relief. Everyone hoped his bad mood would soon end. Once Duke was able to fly again, his friends all said, his spirits would improve. Mariah said she doubted it, knowing the source of his discontent.

Mariah also wrote that Duke had never mentioned Tracy or talked about his time in Seattle—but that didn't mean he wasn't thinking about her. Tracy would've been shocked if he *had* said anything. That wasn't Duke's way.

He hadn't forgotten her. She'd wager she was on his mind every minute of every day, the same way he was on hers. Just how long he'd cling to his stubborn pride she could only speculate.

The doorbell chimed. Kids already? She picked up the candy bowl and answered her door.

Two goblins smiled up at her and screeched, "Trick or treat!"

"And just who might this be?" Tracy asked, squatting down and letting the two youngsters paw through the bowl filled with boxed raisins and granola bars.

"Thanks, Tracy," her neighbor Marilyn Gardener said as she steered her two daughters down the hallway.

Tracy closed the door and set the bowl on a nearby table. Walking to her fridge, she removed the casserole she'd assembled that morning and popped it in the oven. When Duke did come back, she had a real surprise for him. She could cook. Not just one or two recipes, either, but a whole repertoire. Her mother would be proud of her; Sharon Santiago had raised five daughters, and each had become an accomplished cook—with one exception. Tracy grinned to herself. What could she say? She was a late bloomer. Everything seemed to hit her at once. Until she'd fallen in love with Duke, she'd avoided thinking about marriage—and children. She'd been perfectly content to play the role of indulgent aunt.

Duke. Tracy had a great deal to thank him for. Mostly he'd pulled the wool from her eyes and awakened her to life. Her view had been so narrow, her focus solely on her career. Then she and Duke had crashed, and all the things she'd pushed into the background had suddenly sprung free.

Duke. She'd been so confident he'd return!

Why she'd chosen Halloween as her day of reckoning she couldn't explain. Two weeks was an optimistic estimate, she supposed. It was just that she missed him so much and she'd been positive he missed her, too.

Apparently not.

Struggling against a bout of melancholy, Tracy changed out of her business suit and into jeans and a sweater.

The doorbell chimed, and once more Tracy reached for the bowl and opened the door. More neighbor children, looking for a handout.

No sooner had she closed the door than the bell chimed again. This time, however, it was Duke. "Trick or treat," he said, grinning sheepishly.

All she could do was stare at him.

"Raisins? Granola? Sweetheart, you're going to disappoint those poor kids. They want candy, chocolates, the gooier the better."

Happiness bubbled up inside her. "Oh, Duke!" If he didn't reach for her soon, she was throwing caution to the winds and leaping into his arms.

Without waiting for her invitation, he stepped into her living room and closed the door. The teasing light faded from his deep gray eyes as he studied her.

"Sit," he ordered, and Tracy was in no state to argue. She sank onto the sofa, clutching her hands together in her lap. Once she was seated, Duke began to pace in front of her.

"From the moment we met," he said, "you seemed to be of the opinion that you can do anything a man can do."

"Well, for the most part I can," she returned evenly.

"As you've taken great delight in proving to me," he muttered. "Well, surprise, surprise, Ms. Attorney, there are certain matters best left in the hands of a man."

"If you've come all this way to argue with me, then—"

"I didn't."

She stood. "Then I think—"

"Kindly listen," Duke barked.

Because she was so shocked, she sat back down, snapped her mouth shut and did as he asked.

"When it comes to a marriage proposal, you need to learn that a man prefers to do the asking."

Tracy almost swallowed her tongue. "A marriage proposal?"

"You heard me."

"If you're upset about my bringing up the subject first, then you should know I just got tired of waiting. I love you, Duke, and you love me."

"You're doing it again."

She pressed her fingers over her lips. "Sorry."

He continued pacing.

"Well?" she prompted when he didn't immediately speak again.

"Be patient. I'm thinking."

"That's the problem," she insisted, scrambling onto her knees on the sofa. "You think too much." If he didn't stand still long enough to kiss her, she was going to hog-tie him and do the deed herself.

"What makes you think you'll be happy in Hard Luck?" he demanded.

"Because you're there," she answered simply.

He didn't allow her response to sway him. "What about your career?"

"Yes, well, that's a serious consideration, but I've thought it through. I'll set up my own practice. True, there probably won't be enough clients to keep me busy full-time in the beginning, but—"

"At least you're willing to admit it. How do you propose filling your time? I know you, Tracy, and you won't be content sitting on your duff."

"Actually, not having a full-time practice suits my purposes perfectly."

His eyes narrowed. "How's that?"

"I want children, and I believe we should start on the project right away."

Duke's gaze seemed riveted to hers. "Now, just one minute..." He rubbed the back of his neck with his hand as he took in her words. "You really know how to throw a man off center, I'll say that. I haven't so much as proposed, and you're already talking children."

"I want a big family. I had four sisters, you know."

"Lord, woman, would you kindly stop jumping the gun?"

"I'd like three, possibly four of my own and—"

"Four kids, in this day and age?" he said, aghast. "You're not thinking clearly. Couples can't afford to clothe and educate that many children."

"We'll do fine." The man was nothing if not obstinate.

"I haven't agreed to anything yet."

She pretended not to hear him. "I feel it's important that we be young enough to enjoy them."

"Tracy," he said, obviously exasperated.

"Am I answering your questions?"

"You make our marriage sound like a foregone conclusion."

"You mean it isn't?" She batted her eyelashes, teasing him. She'd never be a pliant woman who would easily bend to his will—but for the sake of his ego she supposed she could bend every now and then.

"No way!"

She sighed impatiently. "I'm going to tell our children this, you know."

"Tell them what?"

"That I was the one who proposed."

"The hell you will!"

Tracy nearly laughed out loud. Instead, she held out her arms. "Just how long is it going to take you to kiss me?"

"In a minute," he said, "but first I have to figure out how I'm going to do this."

"Do what?"

He walked over to the sofa and got down on one knee.

Her eyes widened with surprise. Duke was going to propose on bended knee. *Duke?*

"Promise me you won't say a word until I've finished," he instructed.

"I promise," she said breathlessly. Duke was actually going to propose. At last. She pressed her lips together hard to show him her sincerity.

"I didn't want to fall in love with you, and God knows it wasn't what I planned. You're gutsy, stubborn, insolent, hardheaded—and special." His voice lowered to a whisper. "So damn special."

She blinked back sudden tears.

"In addition to all that, you seem to think you love me."

She nodded vigorously. The need to talk was so strong she had to bite her lip.

"I don't know why you love me, but frankly I've given up trying to figure it out. I'm crazy about you. Yes, dammit, I love you. There, I've said it."

She rewarded him by kissing her fingertips and then touching them to his lips.

"I don't know what makes you think you can give all this up for life in Hard Luck, but you seem to have it squared away."

Once more she nodded.

"Three kids, possibly four," he groaned. "Knowing you, you'll probably talk me into ten."

She held up four fingers.

He closed his eyes, shaking his head. "I'm not agreeing to any more than two for now." He paused and grinned. "That's advice a good attorney would give."

She smiled and shrugged. Not speaking was damned difficult, but she'd given her word.

"So you think we should marry."

She held her breath.

"I'm beginning to believe you're right."

Tracy couldn't help it—she threw her arms around his neck and cried joyfully, "Oh, Duke, what took you so long?"

A grimace of doubt tightened his face. "I'm not good enough for you—"

"Don't you dare say that," she interrupted heatedly. "You're the best thing that's ever happened to me, Duke Porter, and don't you forget it."

"Me?"

"Without you, I'd have spent the rest of my days defending my rights as a woman, pushing love out the door, arguing until I had no voice left while standing on my soapbox. Without you, life would've passed me by. I would've missed so many pleasures. I would've been so lonely." She paused, her eyes solemn. "I've learned that I can have my principles and love, too. I need you, Duke."

He blinked, as if he wasn't sure he should believe her. They faced each other. His love in all its depth shone in his eyes, and it was a reflection of what she felt for him.

"We're going to fight like crazy," he whispered.

"And make love like crazy."

A smile edged up one side of his mouth. "I love you, Tracy, so damn much." His arms circled her waist. He kissed her eyes and nose and cheeks and chin, unable to get enough of her. Her senses reeled; her heart raced.

It'd been so long since he'd last held her. She loved the way his eyes darkened before he kissed her. The way his hands moved gently over her body, and the sound of his voice when he whispered her name.

They were going to be very happy—of that Tracy had no doubt. She'd found her man, and he'd found her. A man to love for the rest of her life.

EPILOGUE

SCOTT O'HALLORAN sat on the floor in front of the fireplace at the Caldwells' lodge. Dinner was over and the adults had gathered in the front room, planning a reception for Duke and Tracy. The other kids were watching a video upstairs; Scott, however, had declined the opportunity to see *Snow White*. He'd decided to stay down here with his dog instead. Eagle Catcher rested peaceably on the braided rug next to him, snoring softly as Scott stroked his fur. With a quiet moment to himself, Scott was considering the changes that had come to Hard Luck since his own arrival a couple of years ago.

"I still can't believe it," he told the husky. "Duke married Tracy." He shook his head, feeling wiser than his years. People tended to think of him as "just a kid"—and he couldn't very well deny it—but he was smarter than some folks seemed to think.

For instance, Scott knew long before his mother and Sawyer did that they were in love. Sawyer had insisted the other bush pilots leave Abbey alone—and then found all kinds of excuses to spend time with her himself. But he'd almost blown it with that flippant marriage proposal. If it hadn't been for Susan and him running away with Eagle Catcher, Scott didn't know *what* would have happened. He didn't like to think about it.

His mom had married Sawyer, and now there was little Anna. When they'd learned Anna was a girl, Scott had been sorely disappointed. He'd wanted a little

brother real bad, but now that she was born and everything, he found he was glad to have another sister. Not
that he'd let Susan know. Susan was a pest. But Anna
was all soft and sweet, and when he held her he felt happy
and proud. Scott hoped for a brother someday, but if that
didn't happen, he'd accept another sister.

After his mother and Sawyer got married, it hadn't
taken him long to figure out how things were between
Charles and Lanni. The day he and Susan had gone
looking for wildflowers with Lanni and encountered the
bear proved exactly how much Charles liked Lanni.

Charles had been so relieved when he found them that
he'd kissed Lanni right then and there. Scott never did
understand why it took them so long to decide to get
married. Lanni had to move away, and then Charles
moped around Hard Luck for weeks until he finally saw
the light.

Scott had felt downright sorry for Charles. He'd
wanted to say something, but he'd overheard his parents
talking, and they seemed to think it was best to let
Charles and Lanni sort out their differences themselves.
They must've been right, because not too long after that,
Scott learned Charles and Lanni were getting married the
following spring.

Eagle Catcher stretched out his legs and yawned loudly.
Scott felt tired, too, but he kind of liked sitting here by
the fireplace while the adults talked in the other room.
Duke and Tracy's wedding had taken place in Seattle two
weeks earlier, and they were due back in Hard Luck the
day after tomorrow, so folks wanted to give them a special welcome.

He had to admit those two had taken him by surprise.
But Mitch and Bethany hadn't. Scott smiled to himself.
He'd seen the look that came into his teacher's eyes
whenever Mitch stopped by the schoolhouse. It was the

same look he'd seen in his mother's eyes after Sawyer kissed her the first time.

Susan and Chrissie, Mitch's daughter, had played matchmaker—and it had worked, not that Scott approved of their methods. To his way of thinking, Mitch had married Bethany despite Susan and Chrissie's schemes. They all seemed happy, though. From what he understood, Bethany's baby was due a couple of months before Lanni's. At this rate, the Hard Luck School was going to need more than two teachers. Hard Luck was going through a population explosion.

Matt and Karen's little boy was born a week before Anna. Little Clay Caldwell was the apple of his daddy's eye. Yup. And his mother's, too.

Scott felt a little smug about Matt and Karen. He took full credit for those two patching up their relationship. He figured it was his advice that had helped Matt win back Karen's heart.

Not only that, he'd helped Christian and Mariah. He remembered the evening he'd come across Christian sitting on his front porch, looking down in the mouth—like he'd lost his wallet or something. The "something" he'd lost turned out to be his secretary. Scott liked to think he'd helped his uncle that night, but at the time he wasn't sure Christian had heard a word he'd said. Now Christian and Mariah were married, too, and he suspected it wouldn't be long before they started having children.

Then there were the surprises. First Ben Hamilton and Mrs. McMurphy. Scott hadn't known people that old could fall in love. Ben's behavior—the way he watched Mrs. McMurphy and the way he snapped at everyone— had made him suspicious. He'd talked it over with Eagle Catcher and even his husky friend was skeptical, but Scott knew what he saw. Sure enough, a month later, he heard that Ben and Mary McMurphy were getting hitched.

By this time, Scott had been to more weddings than some ministers. He wondered what kind of bride Mrs. McMurphy would make, seeing that she was practically as old as his grandmother. What surprised him was how pretty she looked. Not pretty the way his mother or Lanni or Mariah were, but different.

Ben, too, although the cook would probably be offended if Scott called him pretty. Ben was a cool kinda guy. Since marrying Mrs. McMurphy he was even more fun. He even let Eagle Catcher into the café now and again, and his cooking was better than ever.

The other surprise came when Scott learned that Duke was marrying Tracy. He'd been worried when their plane went down in a storm. Not just worried about their injuries, but about the two of them killing each other. Boy, had he been wrong. Next thing he knew, Duke was in Seattle visiting Tracy. Now they were married, and Tracy was going to open up a law office in Hard Luck.

Lots of other people were starting new businesses. The last he heard, Pete Livengood was looking to put in a hardware place. There was even talk about a video store—a whole store—not just a few shelves at the back of Pete's grocery. That'd be great. A friend of Karen's from California was moving north to set up a beauty shop, but this would be a place where both men and women got their hair cut. Scott preferred the video store. Oh, and Lanni was starting a newspaper—maybe she'd let him have his own advice column. "Ask Scott," he'd call it. He grinned to himself.

Yup, Hard Luck had changed since the day he arrived. It wasn't just a town fifty miles north of the Arctic any more. Hard Luck was home.

Dear Friends,

This is the end of the road for my Hard Luck family (and they *do* feel like family, every one of them). It's been quite a journey, hasn't it? I don't think I've ever become quite this involved in a project—or had as much fun!

An endeavor of this length can't be accomplished alone. I'd like to give a special word of thanks to my editor, Paula Eykelhof, for her help and encouragement. Editors are some of the hardest-working people I know. Paula put hours of extra work into these stories about the people of Hard Luck, and I appreciate it. I want to thank everyone who contributed to the MIDNIGHT SONS series, especially the following people: Maryan Gibson, whose copyediting expertise we relied on, Wendy Blake Kennish, who lent invaluable assistance of all kinds, and Peter Cronsberry, proofreader extraordinaire, who dedicated extra effort to making sure all the *i*s were dotted and the *t*s crossed. Also Frank Kalan, the talented artist who so beautifully captured the magnificence of Alaska. Thanks, everyone!

And, finally, thanks to all of you who've read this series. I realize many of you are wondering what happens after *Ending in Marriage*. Anticipating this, Lanni O'Halloran (under the guise of my secretary, Renate Roth) is publishing the first edition of the Hard Luck newspaper. If you're interested in a copy, you can write me at P.O. Box 1458, Port Orchard, Washington 98366.

For those of you who've already asked, yes, I'll be writing another six-book series. This time, I'm headed for the Texas plains. I never could resist a cowboy!

Warmest regards,

Debbie

BRIDE'S
BAY RESORT

UNLOCK THE DOOR TO GREAT ROMANCE
AT BRIDE'S BAY RESORT

Join Harlequin's new across-the-lines series, set in an exclusive hotel on an island off the coast of South Carolina.

Seven of your favorite authors will bring you exciting stories about fascinating heroes and heroines discovering love at Bride's Bay Resort.

Look for these fabulous stories coming to a store near you beginning in January 1996.

Harlequin American Romance #613 in January
Matchmaking Baby by Cathy Gillen Thacker

Harlequin Presents #1794 in February
Indiscretions by Robyn Donald

Harlequin Intrigue #362 in March
Love and Lies by Dawn Stewardson

Harlequin Romance #3404 in April
Make Believe Engagement by Day Leclaire

Harlequin Temptation #588 in May
Stranger in the Night by Roseanne Williams

Harlequin Superromance #695 in June
Married to a Stranger by Connie Bennett

Harlequin Historicals #324 in July
Dulcie's Gift by Ruth Langan

Visit Bride's Bay Resort each month wherever
Harlequin books are sold.

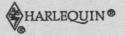

HARLEQUIN ®

BBAYG

MILLION DOLLAR SWEEPSTAKES

No purchase necessary. To enter, follow the directions published. For eligibility, entries must be received no later than March 31, 1998. No liability is assumed for printing errors, lost, late, nondelivered or misdirected entries. Odds of winning are determined by the number of eligible entries distributed and received.

Sweepstakes open to residents of the U.S. (except Puerto Rico), Canada and Europe who are 18 years of age or older. All applicable laws and regulations apply. Sweepstakes offer void wherever prohibited by law. This sweepstakes is presented by Torstar Corp., its subsidiaries and affiliates, in conjunction with book, merchandise and/or product offerings. For a copy of the Official Rules (WA residents need not affix return postage), send a self-addressed, stamped envelope to: Million Dollar Sweepstakes Rules, P.O. Box 4469, Blair, NE 68009-4469.

SWP-M96

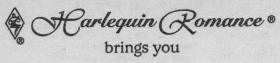

Harlequin Romance ®

brings you

How the West Was Wooed!

We've rounded up twelve of our most popular authors, and the result is a whole year of romance, Western style. Every month we'll be bringing you a spirited, independent woman whose heart is about to be lassoed by a rugged, handsome, one-hundred-percent cowboy!

Watch for...

- May: THE BADLANDS BRIDE—Rebecca Winters
- June: RUNAWAY WEDDING—Ruth Jean Dale
- July: A RANCH, A RING AND EVERYTHING—Val Daniels
- August: TEMPORARY TEXAN—Heather Allison

Available wherever Harlequin books are sold.

HITCH-4

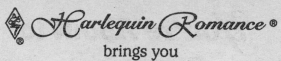
Harlequin Romance ®

brings you

Some men are worth waiting for!

They're handsome, they're charming but, best of all, they're single! Twelve lucky women are about to discover that finding Mr. Right is not a problem—it's holding on to him.

In May the series continues with:

#3408 MOVING IN WITH ADAM
by Jeanne Allan

Hold out for Harlequin Romance's heroes in coming months...

♦ June: **THE DADDY TRAP**—Leigh Michaels

♦ July: **THE BACHELOR'S WEDDING**—Betty Neels

♦ August: **KIT AND THE COWBOY**—Rebecca Winters

HOFH-5

5-2005 KSFB

You're About to Become a
Privileged Woman

Reap the rewards of fabulous free gifts and
benefits with proofs-of-purchase from
Harlequin and Silhouette books

Pages & Privileges™

It's our way of thanking you for
buying our books at your
favorite retail stores.

Harlequin and Silhouette—
the most privileged readers in the world!

For more information about Harlequin and
Silhouette's PAGES & PRIVILEGES program call the
Pages & Privileges Benefits Desk: 1-503-794-2499

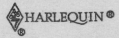

HARLEQUIN ®

BHR-PP125